CHUPACARTER

AND THE HAUNTED PIÑATA

Also by George Lopez and Ryan Calejo

ChupaCarter

CHUPACARTER

AND THE HAUNTED PIÑATA

GEORGE LOPEZ

WITH
RYAN CALEJO

ILLUSTRATED BY
SANTY GUTIÉRREZ

VIKING

VIKING
An imprint of Penguin Random House LLC, New York

First published in the United States of America by Viking,
an imprint of Penguin Random House LLC, 2023

Visit us online at PenguinRandomHouse.com.

Library of Congress Cataloging-in-Publication Data is available.

Printed in the United States of America

ISBN 9780593466001

1st Printing

LSCH

Design by Opal Roengchai
Text set in Athelas

To the moon—thank you

—G. L.

To all the teachers and librarians out there—

muchísimas gracias!

—R. C.

To everyone who (knowingly or not)

pushed me to be better

—S. G.

CHAPTER 1

So there we were, about half the kids in town staring down at a freaky fiery message blazing in the middle of a huge cornfield. A message which—oh, by the way—had quite possibly *probably* been left by, I kid you not, a haunted piñata monster.

It definitely wasn't the kind of thing you saw every day. In fact, it was exactly the kind of thing you hope to *never* see. Unless, of course, you happen to have some weird obsession with fire or the paranormal, but that's a whole other conversation.

That's not me, in case you're wondering. That's Panicky Pete. I don't really know the kid, but he goes to my school and supposedly flips his lid over just about anything. You should hear the stories about him in the lunch line on Mystery Meat Thursdays...

That's me. There in the back. Looking all chulo in my Dodgers ball cap and gray hoodie.

My name is Jorge Lopez, and I'm just your typical Southern California kid. Born and raised in L.A. Throw a wicked curveball. Recently became besties with a chupacabra named Carter.

Okay, so maybe the whole befriending-a-chupacabra thing isn't so typical. Then again, Boca Falls, New Mexico, isn't your typical small town.

Seriously. What kind of place has a spooky, half-burned-down husk of a mansion as its unofficial kid hangout? And how many towns can say they're being haunted by the vengeful spirit of some übercreepy rich kid now trapped in what basically amounts to a cardboard candy dispenser? Not many.

¡Órale! Almost forgot. The übercreepy rich kid— *Miguel Valdez Blackbriar* . . . I probably should've led with him. Y'know, 'cause context and all that.

I mean, how are you supposed to get all terrified by the super freaky fiery message when you don't even know the super freaky backstory?

Oh, and did I mention that the flames were *green*? Yeah. Just a spooky sidenote.

Anyway, so that you can be *properly* terrified, please fasten your seat belts and hold on tightly to the handrails as I rewind us exactly diez minutos . . .

CHAPTER 2

TEN MINUTES EARLIER . . .

"It's probably the scariest town legend in a town full of scary legends," Liza said as the three of us made our way along the vine-choked path through the Blackbriar woods. All around us huge ancient trees rose up, their trunks black with mildew, their roots twisted with age. A silver sliver of moon peeked down at us, filling the woods with a ghostly bluish light.

"I'm scared already," I said jokingly.

Liza's pearly whites flashed in the dark. "You should be. Because it all happened right up there. Up on the highest hill at the very highest point of Boca Falls. But what makes this urban legend *particularly* scary is that it's true. Most of what I'm about to tell you *actually* happened. It's up to you to decide which parts are fact and which parts are fiction."

"The legend starts thirty-six years ago," Liza began, dropping her voice like she was telling a scary campfire story. "The year the Blackbriar family moved to Boca Falls and built themselves the most lavish, most *extravagant* mansion the town had ever seen. The Blackbriars were industrialists, I think, and super wealthy. Rumor is they got rich off steel mills and textiles."

"Some people say it was steel mills and cat hammocks," Ernie interrupted.

Liza shot him a sharpish look. "Yeah, some people say that. But how they got rich doesn't really matter. What really matters is that they had a son, an only child—*Miguel Valdez Blackbriar*." Her voice grew even more ominous now. "He was supposed to be an evil little snotball, too. They say he liked to entertain himself by squashing lizards on his morning walk to school."

"Qué asco," I said, totally grossed out.

"Yep. Yucko *squared*. And as you can probably imagine, his reptile-crushing ways and decidedly prickly personality didn't exactly earn him a seat at the cool kids' table. As a matter of fact, only a couple kids in school would even talk to him."

"Let me guess," I said. "He eventually got fed up and put a curse on his homeroom class, turning everyone into frogs?"

Liza grinned. "Some people would've probably preferred that, actually. No, see, at that point, Miguel was still the new kid in town and really wanted his classmates to like him. He wanted friends. And since his birthday was coming up, he had his parents throw him a birthday party. But not just any old birthday party, mind you. He had them throw the birthday party to *end* all birthday parties. I'm talking jugglers, acrobats, stilt walkers—you name it, they packed them into the grand ballroom of their massive mansion, and then they filled the place with enough balloons, chandeliers, and gilded fun house mirrors to make your head spin. I mean, it was the kid's thirteenth birthday, and he really wanted to impress. He invited everyone, the entire school. But here's the rub: not a *single* kid agreed to go."

"*Nobody?*" I asked. Geez, that had to sting a little.

"Nadie. See, everybody in town thought the Blackbriars were super creepy. Creepy with a capital *C*. And not just Miguel, either. His entire family. Even their servants. But it wasn't long before some of the local kids came up with an idea. A plan—or shall I say, a *prank*."

"What kind of prank?"

"Arguably the sneakiest, meanest, most *diabolical* prank ever pulled in New Mexico! And their first step: trick Miguel. They told him that they'd changed their minds about the party. That they were all now dying to go. And Miguel, of course, couldn't have been happier. He thought he was making new friends. But then, on the big day, the day of Miguel's big birthday bash, they unleashed their *master prank*.

"Instead of singing 'Happy Birthday' and cheering Miguel on while he blew out his candles and opened presents, the kids began singing 'Nighty Nighty, Little Mikey,' a song they had written just for the occasion. No one really remembers the exact lyrics. But whatever they were, I can promise you they weren't very nice. Then, just like they'd all planned, every single kid—all one hundred plus—walked right out of the party, taking Miguel's presents and leaving him all alone, with tears burning in his eyes and an unspeakable pain in his heart."

"Hold up," Ernie interrupted. "I thought the song they sang was 'Miggy Miggy, Little Piggy'?"

"It doesn't really matter *what* the song was called," Liza snapped at him, clearly getting annoyed. "They could've sung 'Blue Suede Shoes,' for all we know. The point is, they made a huge show of mocking him and then they all walked out, flash mob–style. One of the kids even went as far as busting up Miguel's birthday piñata, a priceless work of art which was given to him by his maternal grandfather, suppos-

edly the greatest piñata maker in all of Mexico."

"Man, that's pretty mean," I said. Even if the kid's favorite pastime really *was* lizard-squashing.

"Now, the exact details of that night are not fully known," Liza continued. "What is known, however, are their *consequences* . . ."

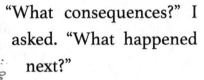

"What consequences?" I asked. "What happened next?"

"Only the fiercest, most *devastating* fire in all of Boca Falls' history!"

I blinked. "Seriously?"

"Cross my heart." Liza made an X over her SAVE THE POLAR BEARS T-shirt. "According to local reports—I'm talking verifiable newspaper articles and eyewitness reports—the old Blackbriar estate blazed like a Viking funeral pyre for nearly an entire *week*. A whole *six* days! The firefighters just couldn't manage to put out the flames. They were unlike anything they had ever seen. Some people say the fire burned so fiercely you could see it on Google Earth."

"Wait. Did they even have Google Earth back then?"

Liza shrugged. "I guess."

"Hold up, though. You never said *how* the fire started."

"Ah, well, like most urban legends, the *how* depends entirely on *who* you ask. But the way most people say it went down was that after the birthday prank, Miguel Blackbriar flew into a fit of uncontrollable rage. And his parents—like most parents probably would—tried everything they could to console him. They immediately ordered every single member of their waitstaff to go buy gifts for their humiliated son, new gifts, anything to cheer him up. But it was too little, too late. Before the servants could return with the presents, Miguel had already thrown everyone out of the ballroom. His mom, his dad, all the performers—everybody. Then he ripped down the decorations, broke all the mirrors, flipped every single table, and flung his birthday cake, *splat*, against the wall, without even bothering to blow out the candles. And it was those very candles—thirteen in total—that legend claims started the fire."

"Tell Jorge what happened next!" Ernie hissed. "Tell him! Tell him already!"

"What happened next," said Liza, "was that a few of the prankers who were on their way home noticed the smoke—the huge black columns billowing from the top of the hill. But by the time they'd made it back up there, there was nothing they could do. The flames were too hot, too intense! They couldn't get within *twenty yards* of the house where Miguel and his parents were now trapped! But one

kid claimed to have heard Miguel's last words—"

"I will have my revenge!" Ernie suddenly shrieked, doing what I guessed was his best Miguel Blackbriar impersonation. "I will have my revenge on this entire town! BOCA FALLS WILL BURN!"

Liza glared at him. "Do you want to tell the story?"

Ernie's hands went up in a "my bad" sort of gesture and he shook his head. "No, sorry. You're doing great. Please continue."

"Anyway," Liza went on, "here's where the creepiness factor *really* kicks up. According to legend, that night, in the midst of the fiercest, scorchiest flames— right smack in the middle of the grand ballroom— somehow, someway, all of Miguel's meanness, all

his cruelty, all of his un-quenchable rage—even his very *soul*!—went into the piñata."

"Wait, wait, wait," I cut in. "What do you mean, 'went into the piñata'?"

"Exactly what I said," answered Liza. "It all went *into* the piñata . . . Miguel *possessed* it!"

Oh, wow. Okay. Now *that* was pretty creepy . . .

I maybe might've sort of shivered a bit as we walked on through the shadowy woods, passing beneath the spidery lacework of branches.

Wish Carter was still in town, I thought. It would've been nice to have a seven-foot-tall bloodsucking chupacabra bodyguard around right about now. By the way, if you don't know what a chupacabra is, just imagine Count Dracula and Sasquatch had a baby. On second thought, *don't* image that. Because it's pretty gross. Just think Chewbacca from Star Wars with a *slight* hankering for goat blood, and you'll get the idea. Oh, and don't forget the deadly, razor-sharp fangs . . .

"Up to this point," Liza said, "some of what I've told you is legend and some is fact. What's not legend, however—what's undisputed *fact*—is that no member of the Blackbriar family—not the mother, not the father, and especially not evil little Miguel—were ever seen again. Their bodies were never found."

But, of course, she told me anyway. "Tons of people claim to have *seen* Miguel. They claim to have seen him, in piñata form, right here in these woods! The Blackbriar woods, as they're still known."

"W-who claims to have seen him?" Ernie asked with an audible gulp. It sounded like he wasn't too familiar with that part of the legend.

"Back when this all happened, at least six different people claimed to have seen the piñata monster," Liza told him. "Almost every member of the Blackbriars' waitstaff and some close friends and family members."

"Hold up," I said. "So none of their maids or butlers or whatever got trapped in the fire?"

"No. The Blackbriars sent them out to buy gifts for Miguel, remember? By the time they got back, the manor was already blazing."

"And no one believed them, right? About the piñata sighting?"

"Nope. At the time, everyone just assumed they'd all gone a little screwy. That they'd lost their minds because of the tragedy. But get this: Not three weeks later, they began to disappear. One after another. The maid. The butler. Miguel's uncle. All of them. They straight-up vanished. And not one of them has ever been seen or heard from since."

"Wait, is that part fact or legend?" I asked, hoping very much that it was the second one.

"One hundred percent cold, hard *fact*."

¡Órale! This is why I never liked small towns! The creepiest stuff ALWAYS happens in small towns.

Suddenly wishing I was back in L.A., I asked, "So w-what'd they say the piñata looked like?" But the moment I'd asked it, I sort of wished I hadn't.

"Please, don't tell us," Ernie squeaked. "It's too creepy out here! I don't wanna be reminded!"

Liza raised her arm again and her phone's glow lit her face from below, casting a mask of eerie bluish shadows over her grinning features.

"They describe the piñata as a *monster*..." she said darkly. "A papier-mâché *ABOMINATION*! Charred black as night, and stinking of fire and boiled licorice, with eyes that blaze the color of poisoned Granny Smith apples!"

And suddenly—

CHAPTER 3

I'm not gonna lie: I came *awfully* close to coloring my undies right then.

I mean, how would you react if you were listening to a scary story about a haunted, fire-breathing piñata monster and then it suddenly appeared right in front of your face?

Exactly.

On the bright side, at least it wasn't the real deal, because in that case, colored undies would've been the least of my worries.

It was actually Team Beetle-Brains: Zane and one of his jock buddies. Two of them were hiding in a tree, probably scaring everyone who came up this way with that ridiculous pink-and-yellow dollar store piñata.

"Jerks!" Liza snapped as she marched right past them, Ernie hot on her heels.

I was feeling super mature, so I punched their stupid piñata in its stupid face, said something my mom would've probably washed my mouth out with soap for, and then strutted off like Steph Curry after sinking a buzzer beater.

"Hope you three losers brought a change of underwear!" Zane shouted after us, and, naturally, the two caveman amigos both burst out laughing and smacked hands. *Dill weeds.*

Ahead of us, the path curved slightly westward and the ground sloped sharply upward like a set of rocky, weed-covered steps. I followed Liza and Ernie into a wall of spindly bushes, and when we emerged out the other side . . . *bam*, there it was. Looming right up in front of us like something out of a scary movie.

Blackbriar Manor.

The mansion itself was clearly off limits. There were KEEP OUT signs all over the walls and windows, padlocks on the doors big enough to keep King Kong out, and a tall barbed wire fence for those who just couldn't take a hint.

But the grounds surrounding the mansion looked like the site of some big traveling fair or something. Just eyeballing it, I'd say there were close to two hundred chamacos out there, all shouting and laughing, roasting marshmallows in the circle of bonfires, and chasing each other around with flashlights and homemade piñatas.

According to Liza, every six years, on the anniversary of the Blackbriar fire, all the Boca Falls kids come out to have a sort of very merry, very *scary* time. It was super weird, I know. But like I said, *small towns* . . .

"Anyway," Liza continued, "legend has it that every six years, Miguel Blackbriar, now in his piñata form, emerges from these very woods to take his revenge on the town below."

"His 'revenge' . . . ha." I glanced over at Ernie, giving him a major eye roll. "And people actually still buy that?"

"Yeah, Jorge!" he snapped. "'Cause it still happens! The fires always start up again—every six years!"

"For real?" I asked, turning to Liza.

She nodded. "Uh-huh. People's fields and houses burn down. Businesses go up in flames. I know a few folks who've even packed up and left Boca for fear that they might be next." She gave a little shrug. "Obviously, most people aren't *that* superstitious. Most don't really believe that the fires have anything to do with the old Blackbriar curse. But when things start burning, people around here tend to get pretty worked up."

As we hoofed it toward Casa del Creepy, a cold wind kicked up and went moaning over the hilltop. I found myself huddling a little deeper into my hoodie.

Liza noticed. Grinning, she teased, "You're not *scared*, are you, Jorge? I mean, it's just a silly legend, after all."

"Me? Scared? Liza, I'm Mexican. The only thing that scares us is gringos trying to make guacamole. And our grandmothers. That's it." Well, that was *mostly* it.

A red-haired girl flying one of those donkey kites dashed past us, chased by two other girls. I watched them for a few seconds as they raced around the largest of the bonfires, duck-duck-goose style, and then I shrugged and said, "No offense, but this is one *creepy* tradition you all got going on down here."

Liza made a face like, *Yeah, kinda . . .* "But tradition is tradition, right? And it's not like anyone ever goes *inside* the mansion or anything . . . at least not since the McDougal triplets went missing way back when."

¡Caramba! Missing triplets now! This story just got creepier and creepier.

"Oh, look! S'mores!" shouted Ernie, his eyes lighting up like a Christmas tree. "Anyone else feel a craving coming on?"

"Sure," I said. "Why not?" Hey, what better way to melt the heebie-jeebies away than with some chocolatey, graham-cracker-y goodness?

We crossed the weedy, overgrown lawns (which were about as long as a football field, and twice as wide) and had just gotten close enough to get a big ole delicious whiff of melty chocolate and ooey gooey marshmallows when a scream ripped the night.

For the span of several heartbeats, everyone froze, every single eye in every single face searching frantically for the source of the scream.

But suddenly, that one scream turned into two. Then three. Then dozens and dozens, and I saw a whole mess of kids spring to their feet like jackrabbits and go racing off toward the edge of the rocky cliff.

"W-what's going on?" Ernie asked anxiously.

Liza shook her head. "No idea. Let's check it out!"

And there you go. The super creepy backstory of the super creepy fiery message. Okay, now let's fast-forward again . . .

So, yeah. That fire was *supposedly* the handiwork of Miguel Valdez Blackbriar, aka the haunted piñata. And did the whole thing make me a *tad* bit uneasy? You bet it did. In fact, there probably wasn't a phone that hadn't dialed for Mommy within three hundred yards!

And fear, just so you know, is probably the most contagious thing on the entire planet. Even more contagious than a bad case of cooties in elementary school, and we all know how fast an outbreak of those can spread.

On the other hand, did I seriously believe that some candy-stuffed papier-mâché party accessory was behind it? No way!

Truth was, I never really believed in ghosts or ghouls or goblins or any other of that paranormal mumbo jumbo. And I *especially* didn't believe in haunted piñatas.

Though, to be fair, I hadn't believed in chupacabras either, and look how wrong I'd been on that one.

Anyway. Little did I know, before the week was up, I'd never look at piñatas the same way again either.

CHAPTER 4

After the übercreepy cornfield message, the vast woods and hilltop surrounding Blackbriar mansion cleared out faster than you could say "haunted piñata!" And yeah, I know you can say "haunted piñata" pretty fast. It was *that* fast.

At any rate, it was almost 7:30 by the time I got home and found my grandparents doing their usual grandparent-y stuff—my abuela reading *Latina* magazine, my abuelo yelling at some overly dramatic telenovela actors on TV.

My grandparents are actually pretty funny. Especially my grandma. The thing to know about her is that she's always negative. She doesn't just see the cup half empty—she sees it chugged down, toweled dry, and then smashed to bits on the kitchen floor.

For instance, last week I asked her if she'd seen

the neighbor's cat and she said, "What happened? It died?" Uh, *no*, the cat hadn't died. It had just had kittens. Then a few days later I said, "Grandma, I'm going over to Ernie's," and she said, "What happened? He died?"

That was how her mind worked. Always the worst-case scenario. Other than that, though, she was cool.

At least when she wasn't yelling at me, or hassling me about chores, or chasing me around the house with her chancla shouting, "¡Huye, cobarde!"

My abuelo seemed pretty caught up in his soap opera at the moment, so I decided to talk to Paz. "Grandma," I said, "do you believe in ghosts?"

And with the way her face twisted up at me, you'd think I'd squirted a chorro of lemon juice in her eye. "¿Qué?" she snapped.

"You know, scary paranormal stuff. Like, haunted houses or whatever."

"Haunted houses are rich people problems," she said, waving a hand dismissively. "How many ghosts you ever heard of who would choose to haunt some little two-bedroom shack in the middle of nowhere instead of some big fancy mansion on Park Avenue?"

Fair point. "So that type of stuff doesn't frighten you?"

"Frighten me? Why would it frighten me? Hey, don't you remember the time I came to visit you and your mom in California, and I went all Kung Fu Panda on that four-legged apparition that snuck up on me while I was frying chimichangas?"

"That wasn't an apparition!" I shouted. "I told you

28

this already! That was PACO, our neighbor's albino *Chihuahua!*"

"Really?"

"YES! And to this day, he still pees himself whenever he sees someone pick up a spatula, thanks to you!"

"Huh. Well, that does explain the ratty little tail..." Paz said thoughtfully. "Still! Serves that ankle-biter right, sneaking up on me like that!"

I sighed. *Geesh.* "Look, whatever. I just want to know what you think about the haunted piñata curse. You know, the old town legend? Because there was this huge fiery message out near the Blackbriar mansion, and everybody seemed pretty scared."

Clapping the magazine shut on her lap, she cried, "I can't believe this! On top of all the other things wrong with you, now you're a scaredy-cat afraid of some silly town *leyenda*? That's what you get for hanging out with kids all the time!"

"I *am* a kid!" I shot back.

"Then maybe it's about time you GROW UP!"

Bah! This lady was impossible! Why did I even bother? "I'm going to go change for dinner," I said, stomping past her while my abuelo practically dropped to his knees in front of the television, pleading, "YOU LOVE ESTEBAN! ESTEBAN IS THE RIGHT MAN FOR YOU! OPEN YOUR EYES, NIÑA!"

"You go 'head and change," I heard my abuela call after me. "But be careful. I think I might've seen a haunted rubber ducky swimming in your bathtub!"

CHAPTER 5

My abuela had made one of her not-so-world-famous specialties for dinner: burnt black bean enchiladas with a side of rock-hard yucca fries. Obviously I wasn't the biggest fan of her "cuisine," but I was even less of a fan of starving to death, so I scarfed down an enchilada, chased it with a slice of flan I'd found hidden in the fridge, then brushed my teeth and got ready to count some ovejitas.

Honestly, I was exhausted.

You'd be surprised how much a good scare can take out of you.

But before climbing into bed, I dragged the big wooden dresser over, butting it up against my bedroom door.

Now, did I seriously think that would be enough

to stop a vengeful, fire-spitting haunted piñata?

No. But at least it was something, right?

About an hour later, I was web-slinging my way through a forest of skyscrapers in downtown NYC, in the process of rescuing Mary Jane from the clutches of some weird, bad guy blend of Dr. Octopus and my horrible ex-principal, Mr. Skennyrd, when I was jerked awake by a strange scr-scr-scratching sound.

It was coming from my window. And at first, I was all like, *No biggie. It's just Mother Nature. Most likely a tree branch.*

But then I remembered that there *were* no trees outside my window—so no branches, either. And that Mother Nature wasn't exactly known for sneakily opening people's bedroom windows in the middle of the night—which, by the way, was *EXACTLY* what was happening right now!

¡LA PIÑATA! shrieked a panicky voice in my head. *IT'S THE HAUNTED PIÑATA!*

Sitting bolt upright, I quickly snapped on the Hello Kitty nightlamp on my bedside table (don't ask) and—

Then, realizing who it was, I gasped, *"CARTER?!"*

The chupacabra showed me some more teeth (and the bits and pieces of whatever he'd had for dinner stuck in between them). "Jorge!"

I blinked up at him, hardly able to believe my eyes. Not only was Carter the first sangre-slurping cryptid I'd ever met, he also happened to be my best friend in the whole wide world! We'd met when I first moved out here from L.A., up on my grandparents' roof, and he helped me get over a pretty tough time, too—getting dumped out here by my mom and all. Then, a few weeks ago, Liza and Ernie had helped me sneak him onto a train headed for Mexico, so he could reunite with his familia (oh, and avoid being turned into office decor by my dream-haunting ex-principal). But apparently the big guy was back!

"Dude, you scared the living *daylights* out of me!" I said, throwing my arms around his furry, beanpole-thin body.

"But . . . it's *night*time." Carter sounded confused. "What daylights?" Which, of course, was classic Carter and totally made me lol.

A split second later, I heard a soft *bang* followed by the shuffle of running feet, and my grandma came bursting into the room, plowing right through my anti-piñata barricade and nearly toppling the whole thing over.

She was armed to the teeth, her "deadly" chancla in one hand, my grandpa's leather cinto dangling, whip-like, in the other; and with her brown pajama pants, brown cardigan, and dark brown nightcap, she almost had an abuela Indiana Jones vibe going on.

"¿QUÉ PASÓ?" she screamed at me, her dark eyes sweeping the room.

I gestured back at Carter like, *Duh. What do you think happened?* And then realized, oh snap, the over-grown mosquito had disappeared under my bed!

I guess he didn't like the idea of squaring off against an angry, fully armed Paz. Couldn't exactly blame him there.

"Don't just sit there, dummy!" my sweet old nana roared at me. "What the heck was all that screaming about?"

"I, uh . . . had a nightmare," I lied.

"A nightmare? What NIGHTMARE?"

"I dreamed there was a . . . *monster* under my bed." Ha! See what I did there?

"Well, keep your nightmares to yourself!" snapped Paz. "And if you ever scream like that again, you better *pray* there's a monstruo under your bed, because if I have to come back in here, I'm kickin' SOME-THING'S butt!"

"Love you too, Grandma!" I called as she slammed the door behind her. Then, when the Cowardly Lion—er, chupacabra—had crawled out from underneath my bed, I blinked up at him and said, "Hold up, are you part of some freaky, enchilada-induced dream?"

"Dude, you're supposed to be in *Mexico*!" I hissed. "In Calle Hueso! What happened?"

All of a sudden, Carter's face fell and his mismatched eyes—one green, the other blue—filled with a sort of lonely gloominess. "No estaban allí, Jorge. They weren't in Calle Hueso."

"You mean your family wasn't there?"

He gave his kangaroo-shaped head a miserable shake.

"Seriously?"

More head shaking. But then an instant later, it was like someone flipped a light switch in his head, because his entire face brightened right up again.

"But I spoke to an elder!"

"Huh?"

"The eldest chupacabra in all of México! It was her idea I come back to Boca Falls. She say to me, very seriously, 'Carter, you must go back to the place you feel is *home*.' And gracias a ti, Jorge, these woods feel more like home than any place I ever known."

"Bro, you're going to make me cry," I said, slinging an arm around my best bud.

I still remembered when Carter told me that, for chupacabras, home wasn't a place; it was a feeling.

And that's because they were migratory animals, always on the move.

Funny thing was, all my life, I'd pretty much been on the move, too, moving from place to place with my mom. I never really felt like I belonged anywhere, either.

But Carter had changed all that for me. He'd made Boca Falls feel like a real home. Which, by the way, is something I would have never even dreamed possible a few months back when my mom sent me out here from L.A. So to hear him say that I'd done the same thing for him was really cool.

"So what's the plan, dude?" I asked, nudging him with my elbow. "What are you going to do about your family?"

"The elder told me she had a dream 'bout dat!" he said excitedly. "She say my family will find me when I go home. But dat makes sense, no? Because if I runnin' around, lookin' for dem, and they back here lookin' for me, we never gonna find each other. And now with the dips gone, I don't put nobody in danger by hanging around."

It was true. The dips *were* gone, and so was Boca's most famous big-game hunter, my school's

Remember these bad boys?

psychopathic ex-principal, Mr. Skennyrd. After his little "heart-to-heart" with Carter in the woods that day, he'd quit his job—and his favorite hobby too, I guess—and run off to join the Defenders of Wildlife organization. Pretty ironic, I know.

"Then your plan is to just . . . *what*? Chill here?" I said. "Wait for your family to find you?"

"Sí. And they *will* find me, Jorge. The elders are never wrong. They very wise. And they always know best. *Always.*"

Apparently chupacabras took the whole "respect your elders" thing to the next level. I'd like to see them try that with Paz as one of their elders. Ha!

"I'm just so happy to have you back!"

We smacked hands again, and hugged it out again, and then his large owl-like eyes blinked down at me while his scaly, howler monkey–like tail began to thud excitedly against the bottom drawer of my dresser. "Hey, you think your grandma will get mad if I sleep here tonight?" he whispered.

I wasn't going to lie to him. "Heck yeah, she'll get mad! Everything makes that lady mad!" Then, flashing him my most mischievous grin: "But what Granny don't know, *Granny don't know . . .*"

CHAPTER 6

That night we could hardly sleep, we were so excited. So we pretty much just lay there, talking about all sorts of things.

Carter told me about his trip down south—the speedy train ride out to Chula Vista and the slow trek back through the southwestern United States—and I told him about what I'd been up to and about that spooky town legend surrounding the Blackbriar family.

We both laughed about the idea of a haunted piñata (and laughed about what kind of candy it might have for guts) but also nearly jumped out of our skins when a sudden hailstorm began pelting the roof.

No joke, it sounded an *awful* lot like some fiendish piñata monster raining down a shower of poisoned candy!

When my alarm clock (aka, my grandma's pot-and-spatula symphony outside my door) jerked me out of sleep early the next morning, Carter was gone. He'd probably slipped out into the woods to "fertil-ize" some shrubs and look around for his family.

It was Monday, a school day, so after breakfast I got my stuff together and headed out the front door. Lately, I'd started walking to school. There were a couple of reasons for that.

One, my grandma had stopped paying the school for bus service. She'd said, and I quote, "I ain't paying for you to have your own *chauffeur*! You might start thinking you're one of those silly rich kids and imagine how big your head will get then!"

Reason number two, even though Paz had repaired her "Chica Mobile" after our little game of bumper cars with Skennyrd and it was looking fresher than ever, she'd recently gotten super into reggaeton, blasting it on her car's ear-busting speaker system every chance she got, and there was *zero* chance I was getting dropped off in front of a bunch of kids my age with my grandmother belting out the words to "Despacito."

As I made my way along the dusty sidewalk, walking past mailboxes and yard signs, I thought about

what I could do to help Carter find his family. A bunch of ideas came to me, but none were very good.

I also found myself thinking about the whole haunted piñata curse, but with the sun out and all the spookiness of last night in the rearview, I couldn't help but laugh about it. I mean, it was silly to think just how worked up everyone had gotten over some ridiculous cornfield fire and a silly town legend.

Fact: the fiery message had been nothing more than a prank. Probably just a couple of chamacos with a few matches and a lot of time to burn.

How could I be so sure? Easy. Because there were no such things as haunted piñatas or fire-breathing monsters, and there *certainly* wasn't any such thing as a fire-breathing haunted piñata monster! I mean, chupacabras were one thing. But evil, undead candydispensers set on fiery revenge? Gimme a break ...

I was still laughing about it as I hopped over the train tracks in the middle of town. But the moment I turned the corner onto Main Street, I realized that I might've been the *only* one laughing about it ...

Everywhere I looked, I saw fear. It was practically

stamped on every face. It made every hand tremble, and every eye dart anxiously about.

The entire street was deathly silent, too. I got the impression that if I would've yelled "BOO!" the whole town would've gone running off in terror. It was like they were all genuinely afraid of that ridiculous Blackbriar legend. I just didn't get it.

No big surprise, things weren't much different at my school. Most of the kids huddled in nervous packs around water fountains and fire alarms, and hardly anybody talked as we waited for the first period bell to ring.

On my way to homeroom, I spotted two fourth graders wearing firefighter jackets about five sizes too big for them, and even saw one girl wearing a fire extinguisher in place of a backpack!

At lunch, I found Ernie and Liza sitting at our usual spot by the vending machines. I came up behind E-dog real chill—like I always did—but apparently today it wasn't chill enough. He whirled wildly around, sending a forkful of macaroni arcing through the lunchroom, then quickly leveled the business end of his *Star Trek* phaser pen on me with shaking hands.

"*Set phasers to stun!*" he shrieked.

"Dude, please don't tell me you're scared of a make-believe, candy-stuffed donkey, too," I said, honestly starting to get a little annoyed by the whole thing.

Ernie gulped. Tried to, anyway. Which pretty much answered my question. "This is no time for jokes, Jorge! We're dealing with some seriously scary stuff here!"

Sliding in beside him, I glanced across the table at Liza,

who looked like her typical calm, cool, and collected self as she worked through what was probably next year's math homework. "Well, if it's so scary, how come you're not shaking in your hundred percent faux-leather kicks?"

"Why would I be?" she asked all nonchalantly, swapping her pencil for a forkful of purple tofu. "Some of us aren't *five* anymore."

She shot Ernie a real mean-ingful look. But its

meaning just deflected off the side of his head.

Liza said, "That so-called *warning* in the cornfield last night was obviously a hoax. An elaborate hoax, but a hoax nonetheless. The fact is, I've yet to see a shred of scientific evidence suggesting the existence of any paranormal entity anywhere in Boca Falls. Much less the existence of some *haunted piñata*."

"Hey!" Ernie hissed. "Don't say that out loud!"

"Don't say what? Haunted piñata?"

"*STOP*, Liza! It might"—and this part he whispered—"*hear* you."

Liza groaned, showing him the bottoms of her eyeballs. "It's a piñata, Ernie. Not Bloody Mary. It's not going to *magically* appear because we say 'haunted piñata' three ti—"

Suddenly, what looked like a giant flaming *meteor* came crashing down on the table in front of us with a sizzling *whoosh*!

A bunch of kids let out shrieks of horror-movie-level terror. Ernie and I both leapt out of our seats,

Ernie screeching, "TH-TH-THE HAUNTED PI-
ÑATA!"

Then, from behind us,
came a howl of laughter,
and the excited smack-
ing of hands, and it
took me all of two sec-
onds to realize that the
"flaming meteor" wasn't
really a meteor, and it certainly
wasn't a haunted piñata monster.

What it was: a lunch tray.

Confused, my heart slamming against my ribs,
I looked frantically around and yep, there was the
entire Bozos "R" Us crew standing right behind us,
and having a great time, too—all of them laughing
so wild and uncontrollably that tears were streaming
down their pimply, pockmarked faces.

"Bunch of overgrown cucarachas!" I shouted at
them.

Zane Zagorski, the undisputed king of all jock
bozos everywhere, gave me his trademark evil grin.
Zane was the prototypical middle school bully-jerk.

He was captain of the soccer team, dished out wedgies like they were going out of style, and practically lived in the detention room. The guy might've been five times the size of your average sixth grader (and, ironically, about half as smart), but I wasn't some *cobarde*. I wasn't about to back down. I'd fought bigger and come out on top. Well, maybe not. But still.

"Easy there, spudz," King Bozo warned me. "This time it was just a lunch tray. But next time it might be your locker that catches fire. Or Madame Cure-all's latest science project." His mean little eyes had flicked toward Liza.

"It's Madame *Curie*," she corrected him, sighing in disgust and putting out the flaming lunch tray with her bottle of Perrier.

"Oooh, *my bad!*" said Zane, like it was the comeback of the century and, of course, he smacked hands with a couple of his goons. Then he was strutting backward, still grinning at me as he led his gang of loyal cavemen toward the cafeteria door. "The fact is, the piñata's back, spudz . . . so I think it would be wise for you to keep your *cool*, don't ya think?"

Geesh. What a total waste of a single brain cell. And some people believe amoebas can only be observed under a high-powered microscope . . .

When Zane and his gang of ignoramuses had made like basketballs and bounced out of the lunchroom, I decided it was probably a good time to drop the big Carter news—y'know, to lighten the mood.

But of course, I didn't just straight-up tell Liza and Ernie. That would've spoiled all the fun. I *hinted* at it. What I actually told them was that I had a huge surprise waiting at my house, and that both of them should come over after school for a "bloody" good time.

Ernie, go figure, was as excited as Pikachu in a thunderstorm. For some reason, he got it into his head that I'd bought a scale model of the USS *Enterprise* from *Star Trek* for us to assemble together, and even though I told him he was way off—like way, *waaay* off—he kept winking at me and saying that he'd come packing his trusty bottle of Superglue, just in case.

Liza agreed to come over, too, but a little later, because her dad was picking her up right after lunch and she wasn't sure why.

At any rate, I couldn't wait to see the looks on their faces!

CHAPTER 7

It was a little after 4:00 when Ernie showed up at my house.

True to his word, he'd brought along his bottle of Superglue and a wall-size technical deconstruction of Captain Jean-Luc Picard's famous space vessel, which he said we could use for general reference.

"This is no place for such a sacred piece of science fiction history," he told me as I led him across the backyard and out to the stretch of woods that ran along the edge of my grandparents' farm. "Why would you hide the miniature way out here?"

"I don't know about any miniature," I said, "but I've got a *giant* surprise for you!"

Then, just like we'd practiced, Carter leapt out from behind a tree, claws up, fangs bared, in his best horror movie monstruo pose.

The shriek that burst from Ernie's mouth could've shattered glass. But after he'd gotten a grip (and we'd all gotten our hearing back—*yeesh!*), he shouted, "CARTER!" and threw his arms around everybody's favorite bloodsucker.

E-dog whirled to face me, wide-eyed with shock. "What's he doing here?!" Then he swung back around to face Carter. "What are you doing here?!"

So Carter and I broke it down for him like a fraction, and when we were finished, he said, "That's awesome! Well, not the you-not-being-able-to-find-your-family part. But definitely the you-being-back part!"

CHAPTER 8

We spent the next half an hour or so chillaxing in the woods, playing catch, and waiting for Liza. But when 5:00 rolled around and she still hadn't shown up, it became pretty obvious that she'd forgotten all about our little playdate.

At that point we tried texting her, calling her, tweeting her, blowing up her Snapchat, and DMing her on Instagram, Twitch, and TikTok, but nothing.

Nada.

Eventually, though, our curiosity got the best of us, and we decided to head over to her house to find out why she'd left us hanging.

Liza didn't live very far, only a couple of miles, and we went the long way through the woods, so Carter could tag along.

When we finally reached her house, we left the

chupacabra waiting in the trees nearby and ran up the wide cement steps of her porch.

But before we could even ring the bell, the front door flew open and out came Lara Croft—well, Liza, *looking* like a real-life Lara Croft.

Hey, you're going to a **Tomb Raider** cosplay party and didn't invite us? Very UNCOOL!

Sighing, Liza gave a big eye roll. "Yes, the shorts and tank are from my *Tomb Raider* costume from two Halloweens ago. But *no*, I'm not going to any cosplay party."

"Oh, yeah?" snapped Ernie. "Well, if you're not going to some super exclusive cosplay party, then where *are* you going, Ms. Fake Croft?"

"I'm going to go look for something."

Look for something? I shook my head. "You were supposed to come over, remember? What happened?"

Liza didn't say anything, but from the way her shoulders slumped and her eyes dropped slowly, almost sadly, to her boots, I could tell something wasn't right.

"What is it?" I said uneasily. "What's wrong?"

And suddenly tears were shining in her eyes. Big, fat, quivering tears. "There was another one," she said, her voice trembling with emotion. "Another fire."

"A fire? Where?"

"At my dad's butcher shop. It burned down!"

CHAPTER 9

"*WHAT?*" Ernie and I blurted in unison. Yep. That was just about the last thing we'd expected her to say.

Liza was wiping at her eyes now, smearing away the tears. "It's gone. Pretty much the entire shop. *Gone.*"

I blinked, feeling like the whole world had suddenly become a giant rug and someone had just as suddenly yanked it out from under me. I mean, I'd just been at her dad's shop two days ago! Shopping for brisket with my abuelita. How could it be gone?

"Liza, that's awful," I said, hardly knowing what to say.

"Totally awful," Ernie agreed.

But then a sudden thought struck me.

"Hold up," I said. "You're not just making this up

because you really *are* going to some awesome cosplay party and don't want to hurt our feelings, right?"

Liza shook her head. "No. It happened early this morning, around 6:00 a.m. My dad didn't even hear about it until after he'd dropped me off at school. The fire department spent most of the day trying to put out the fire. I didn't find out until my dad picked me up. He could barely even look at me, he was so devastated."

By this point, Ernie's eyeballs had expanded to roughly the circumference of the earth. "You—you're saying the haunted piñata burned down your dad's butcher shop?!"

"Of course not!" Liza snapped. "That piñata is just a ridiculous town legend!"

"Don't call it ridiculous!" Ernie hissed. "That could make it angry! It'll strike again!"

"And that's exactly what they'd *like* you to believe!"

"Time out," I said. "Who's *they*? What are you talking about?"

"Isn't it obvious, Jorge? There's an *arsonist* among us. A fire-starting psychopath living in Boca Falls!"

"A psychopath?" Ernie's voice was so high-pitched

and squeaky that you would've thought someone had blasted his vocal cords with a shrink ray. Under different circumstances (i.e., had we not been discussing the possibility of a fire-starting lunatic lurking in our friendly little town), I might've lol'd.

Liza said, "Think about it, Jorge. It's obviously just some twisted arsonist! They've been taking advantage of that stupid legend for the last *three decades* now! Every six years either they start setting fires—or some copycat arsonist does—and every six years the whole town starts going ballistic over what basically amounts to an oversized Pez dispenser! It's how this villain gets their kicks." An edge came into her words as she said, "Whoever burned down my dad's shop isn't some make-believe, papier-mâché party decoration. They're real enough. And I'm going to make sure they *pay* for this."

"B-but what makes you so sure it wasn't an accident?" I asked her.

Liza's sharp gaze locked on mine and her voice was an intense, action movie whisper. "Because the flames burned *green* . . ."

CHAPTER 10

"GREEN FLAMES?!" Ernie burst out, looking like he might pass out on the spot. "You mean, just like the cornfield message?"

When Liza nodded, I asked, "How do you know the flames were green?" and she said, "Because there was an eyewitness."

"For real?"

"Uh-huh. Cathy Olson. She's the manager at the shop, and she'd just moved into the little apartment above it."

"But green flames can only mean one thing!" screeched Ernie. "EVIL PIÑATA MAGIC!"

"Uh, I've got to be honest. I'm starting to lean evil piñata magic, too," I admitted to Liza. Seriously. Like, what else?

Liza groaned, clearly annoyed. "Again, that's *exactly* what they'd like us to believe!"

"Well, mission accomplished," Ernie said, "because I believe it!"

"And that's fine by me. But I'm a woman of science and I'm on my way to prove that these stupid superstitions are nothing more than stupid superstitions!" Then, locking her front door, she started quickly down the porch steps.

"Hey, where are you goin'?" I called after her.

"I'm going to take a look near the shop. Try to find some evidence to support my hypothesis."

"This is no time for nerd speak!" Ernie shouted. "We're obviously dealing with something beyond the limits of science!"

"But isn't looking for evidence the police's job?" I asked Liza.

"It would be," she said, "except that most of the Boca police department and firefighters grew up right here in town, which means they're probably seeing fire-breathing piñata monsters lurking around every corner—just like Captain Jean-Luc Pi*cowardly* over here." She was giving Ernie one of her classic "Off with his head!" type of looks.

"You're going alone?" I asked.

"Nope. I'm bringing my trusty flashlight along." She held it up for me to see.

"What about your dad?"

Liza glanced back toward her house and her mouth drooped into a frown so sad it broke my heart.

"He's too messed up about all this," she whispered. "That store was the last thing he and my mom built together before she . . . she passed away. It meant the world to them. And it still means the world to him. Besides, I'm a big girl. I'll be okay."

Liza put on an I'm-as-hard-as-steel face. But she wasn't fooling me. I saw right through it. See, I'd used that same tough face about a million and one times throughout the years—every time I started wondering about why my dad had ditched my mom and me, every time things got rough at school, and even when my mom sent me away to live with my grandparents. It was just a small piece of armor you could wear on the outside when you felt all weak and broken on the inside.

Anyway, it was clear what I had to do. Liza had been there for me since day one. She'd been nice to me when none of the other kids in school would even talk to me. She was a good friend. No, a *great* friend. And there was nothing—no haunted piñata, no fire-crazed arsonists, *nothing*—that was going to stop me from being a great friend back. Because that's the core of friendship: it's a two-way street.

"Hey, we'll help," I told her. "We're going with you."

"We are?" Ernie squeaked.

"*Yes,*" I said, "because friends always look out for each other. No matter what."

"Even when it's getting dark out and the *what* happens to be an undead killer piñata?"

"*Especially* then," I said.

Ernie hesitated for a moment, then seemed to muster up his courage. "Hey, Jorge's right! We're going with you, Liza! After all, friends don't let friends get eaten by haunted piñata monsters alone, right?" He gave a shaky smile. That had probably sounded a lot better in his head.

"You don't know how much this means to me, guys . . ." Fresh tears shone in Liza's eyes, but this time I was pretty sure they were happy tears. "I don't even know how to say thank you."

Putting an arm around her, I said, "Being besties means you never have to."

CHAPTER 11

Five minutes later, Carter won himself another Oscar for Scariest Surprise by a Seven-Foot-Tall Bloodsucking Cryptid, and Liza's mood kicked up at least ten more notches.

"CARTER!" she screeched with delight. "What are you doing here?"

His lips split in a big grin that was all gleaming fangs and furry charm. "I was in el barrio. Wanted to say hola."

"Oh my gosh, this is an *awesome* surprise!"

As you probably guessed, Liza couldn't have been any happier to see the big guy. But she was obviously super bummed to learn that he hadn't been able to find his family.

Still, she spoke for all of us when she said, "It's

great having you back, though, Carter!"

After all the daps and hugs were exchanged, we got Carter up to speed on what had happened to Liza's dad's shop and explained where we were going. And suffice to say, the big guy was ready to sink his teeth into the case. *Literally*. He promised Liza that we'd find whoever—or *what*ever—was behind the fire and "fang their butts!" I'm guessing that was the chupacabra version of "kick their butts."

On the way over to the butcher shop, Liza gave us the details on exactly what had gone down. The eyewitness she had mentioned, Cathy Olson, claimed to have locked up shop at precisely 5:30 p.m., just like she always did. Then she went upstairs to her apartment where she spent the rest of the night hanging out and watching TV. But at around 4:00 or 5:00 in the morning, a strange sound jerked her out of sleep, and when she went downstairs to investigate, she discovered the fire. She tried to put it out, but the flames were too powerful and spread too quickly. So she called 911 and escaped out into the parking lot, coughing and stumbling and tripping over herself. That's when, according to Cathy, she saw the thing. *The haunted piñata.*

"*Wait*," Ernie said. "So Cathy claims she actually SAW the piñata monster?!"

"Calm down," Liza told him. "There's a perfectly reasonable explanation for that."

"Well, I'd really like to hear that explanation. And reasonably fast, too!"

"It's simple," Liza said. "In life-threatening situations, people claim to see all sorts of incredible things. It's called stress-induced hallucination. Medical professionals have been documenting it for years. It's just a little trick of the mind."

"Hit rewind real quick," I said. "So Cathy *actually* believes she saw the piñata monster?"

"Yes, but she says she saw it only seconds before passing out from inhalation."

"You mean from the smoke?" asked Carter.

Liza nodded. "Yeah. The paramedics found her lying in the middle of the parking lot and she was unconscious all the way to the hospital. Cathy had only been awake for a few hours when I went to see her." Her forehead creased in a puzzled frown. "Honestly, the only part of this that has me confused is how the arsonists got inside the shop in the first place. From what I saw in the official report, Kenneth Ignis— Boca's fire chief—says he believes the fire started inside one of the display stands in the front. But there was nothing in them that could've caused a fire, and even stranger, there were no signs the shop had been broken into. And only Cathy and my dad have keys, so that's where I'm stuck. All the locks were brand-new. State-of-the-art. So how did the arsonist get in?"

"Because it wasn't an arsonist!" Ernie burst out. "It was the haunted piñata monster, and haunted piñata monsters don't *need* keys! It can probably walk right through walls, if it wants to!"

Suddenly, Carter whirled around to face Ernie, tail twitching, furry brows raised in concern. "You really think it can do dat? Walk through walls?"

"It's a haunted piñata!" Ernie answered in a trembling voice. "There's no telling *what* it's capable of!"

CHAPTER 12

When we finally reached the thick stretch of woods by Liza's dad's butcher shop, it must've been close to 7:00, and the moon was a shiny silver nickel in the sky.

All around us, oaks and firs stood like leafy skyscrapers, and a thin ground mist slithered up between them, slipping around our legs like giant dewy snakes. The night was eerily quiet, and the wind had an icy bite to it. Beyond the edge of the woods, through the lacework of branches, I could see the charred remains of the butcher shop.

Now, I've got to be honest: hearing about the fire had been bad. But actually *seeing* it up close like this—seeing the burnt, blackened walls, the busted windows, the charred, caved-in roof (which, by the way, still appeared to be smoldering in places)—was

like a donkey kick to the gut. It was hard to breathe.
It was even harder not to cry.

"I appreciate the sentiment," Liza said, "but piñatas had nothing to do with this."

Just then, a long, shrill cry echoed in the distance.
It was probably just an owl, but that didn't stop
my heart from nearly busting out of my chest and
launching into orbit.

Ernie, Carter, and I all did our best Frosty the
Snowman impersonations and froze. Liza, on the
other hand, just let out a sigh of total annoyance.

"Guys, seriously—*chill*," she said. "We're practically in the middle of town. Like, five minutes from a McDonald's! Just spread out and see if you can find something."

"*Spread out?*" Ernie hissed. "We can't spread out! That's exactly what they always do in scary movies and that's exactly when the monster starts picking them off, one by one, and EATING them!"

"Except there is no *monster* out here that could eat you!" Liza snapped. "Well, except for him, of course," she said, nodding at Carter, and the seven-foot-tall fanged bloodivore sort of shrugged as if to say, *Yeah, can't argue with that.*

A few minutes later, as Lara Croft—er, Liza—began picking carefully through some random spindly shrubs, I came up beside her and asked, "Hey, so what are we doing here?"

And the look she gave me was the kind usually reserved for the person who ate the last potato chip. "I thought I'd made my plans pretty clear, no?"

"What I mean is, why *here*? Your dad's shop is waaay over there. If we're looking for clues, shouldn't we be searching the parking lot, or somewhere closer?"

"Negative. The police would've already found anything worth finding near the shop," she explained.

"Besides, this is the exact spot where Cathy claims to have seen the supposed piñata demon. A fifty-yard straight shot from the front doors."

"Cathy said *this* was the exact spot?" Ernie squeaked.

When Liza nodded, he turned and Usain-Bolted about ten yards back the way we'd come, clicked his heels a couple of times, spat on the ground, did some kind of twirly, swirly circle dance, and then asked if any of us had a saltshaker on our persons. I told him that was a big nope from me.

Ernie said, "Then maybe we should go search for clues someplace else . . . and I mean someplace *really* far away from here!"

"We're not going anywhere, because there *is* no haunted piñata monster!" Liza snapped. "Whatever Cathy thought she saw was obviously something else—and more than likely, the person who burned down my dad's shop. Now would you all *please* spread out and search the area?"

So we did. Reluctantly. But we'd only been playing detective for about a New York minute when, from several yards away, I heard Carter shout, "Ooh! ¡Encontré algo!"

We all rushed over.

"What is it?" I whispered.

Carter's ears twitched excitedly and his long tail stuck straight up like an exclamation point as he gestured eagerly at the ground.

In the bleary glow of Liza's flashlight, I could see a mess of prints in the soft earth. Footprints. *Big* ones.

"¡Huellas!" said Carter, jumping up and down like he'd just hit BINGO! "These animals prints! These *chupacabra* prints!"

CHAPTER 13

Carter wasn't wrong. Those *were* chupacabra foot-prints. But he had overlooked one *itty-bitty* detail . . .

"Bro, those are *your* footprints!" I told him. "Look how they go around in circles exactly where you've been walking!"

Carter blinked a long, slow blink as he took a dip into his think tank. Then his furry features twisted into the same sort of embarrassed look he gave me when I caught him fanging my grandma's wine boxes. "My bad . . . forgot I wasn't wearin' sneakers."

Liza let out a sigh like maybe she was seriously regretting letting us tag along, and we all spread out again.

But not two minutes later, the bipedal bloodhound had sniffed out something else. "Ooh! ¡Mira! *Look!*"

We all rushed over again.

Carter gave it a sniff. "Smells funny."

"That's because it's dead!" I shouted, grossed out to the power of *twenty*. "Now chuck it already, dude!"

I'd barely had time to turn back around when one of Carter's long, bony fingers poked me on the shoulder.

"¡Mira!" he hissed, and I glanced back to see him

still dangling that nasty dead mouse by its nasty dead tail.

"Carter, didn't I tell you to chuck that thing?"

"This not the same ratón," he told me. "This a different one!"

Eh. It might've been, too. On second look, the tail was a bit longer and *a lot* hairier.

"This not natural," the chupacabra said gravely, looking between Ernie and me. "Dey bodies so *stiff*!"

"It *is* kind of creepy," Ernie whispered. "I mean, they almost look Harry Potter–petrified!"

"It's not petrification," I said. "It's called rigor mortis. Now, can you please get rid of that before we all catch the bubonic plague?!"

"Guys, focus!" Liza snapped, pinning us in the glare of her flashlight.

"I *super* focused!" replied Carter. Then, just to prove how focused he was, an instant later his large shining eyes drifted slowly past me, gradually expanding to the size of baseballs, and he shouted, "Ooh! Squirrel!" before bolting off into the woods.

"Where's he goin'?" Ernie rasped.

I just shrugged. "He has a thing for squirrels."

A few minutes later, when the super focused random squirrel chaser finally rejoined the class,

I noticed something odd: the fur around his long muzzle, and on the sides of his head, and at the tips of his pointy ears was . . . *sparkly.*

Honestly, if I didn't know any better, I would've thought he'd just gotten all kissy-face with a glitter bomb!

Liza had noticed it, too. "Carter! What's—?"

"I know, I know," groaned the chupacabra. "I gotta *think* before I act. Jorge always tells me . . . But it's jess so hard when I see those fluffy, flicking tails!"

"No, dude—you're sparkling!" I said. And you'd think I'd just told him that he'd won first place at the local beauty pageant or something.

Suddenly Count Dracula's brother from another mother was posing, squaring his skinny shoulders, and puffing out his bony chest like some king-of-the-yard rooster. Not even the Greek hunter Narcissus would've looked half as pleased with himself as Carter did just then.

"Well, chupacabra fur *is* very beautiful on moon-lit nights like this," he said, practically bursting with pride. "Some have even described it as *dazzling*. And we don't use no special shampoo or nuthin'. It jess comes natural."

"Dude, no. I mean you're *literally* sparkling!" I shouted.

We all hurried over to him, and after about five seconds of checking out the mess of mysterious glittery stuff in his fur, Liza's wide eyes flew left, right, left, and she shouted, "LOOK!"

That explained how Carter had gotten that stuff all over him: while running through the woods, chasing the squirrel!

"C'mon!" Liza said, and we followed Tinker Bell's shimmering trail all the way until the ground sloped steeply up and we reached a stand of thick oaks surrounded by clumps of bull thistle. Here all traces of the glittery stuff vanished as mysteriously as they had appeared.

Shaking her head, Liza stared disbelievingly around, the bright beam of her flashlight bouncing off tree trunks and picking out smooth gray boulders among the weedy tangles.

"I don't get it," she said. "What is that stuff? And why is it only on some of the trees?"

Ernie had joined in on the head shaking, too. "No idea," he whispered.

Then I heard Carter say, "Hey, what are those?"

Every eye in the vicinity followed his clawed pointing finger, and an instant later every jaw dropped. Oh, snap! *Tracks!*

CHAPTER 14

"They look like Rollerblade tracks!" Ernie hissed.

It was true, too. Except . . . "I don't see any side-walks out here. And you can't Rollerblade too well over rocks and twigs."

"They're definitely not tire tracks," Liza said.

"Not animal tracks, either," whispered Carter.

The tracks ran for about ten or so yards, curving off to the west, away from the shop, before disappearing into the thick, bushy undergrowth.

Liza squatted over down in the dark for a closer look. "They look mechanical," she said as she played her flashlight up and down them. "The lines are super perfect. Almost no variation. Definitely machine-made."

"Could it have been giant snakes or something?"

I asked. Yeah, I was reaching. But it was possible, no?

"I don't think so. The tracks run too straight."

Hmm. Good point. No visible slithering action.

"It would have to be a pretty nimble machine to have gotten this deep in the woods," Ernie pointed out.

"And pretty heavy, too," said Liza, reaching two fingers into one of the tracks and not even touching the bottom, "considering the depth of these."

All of a sudden, from somewhere behind us, Carter shouted, "Found something!"

I turned. From where I was standing, it looked like he was holding up—oh, gross!—somebody's snot-rag.

"A hanky!" he shouted. "Issa 'nother clue!"

"That's *not* a clue," I told him. "It's someone's fancy tissue. And it's *used*. Get rid of that nasty mess, dude!"

"But I don't see no boogers..." The leathery end of his nose wrinkled as he delicately sniffed the filthy-looking rectangle. "Smells like *ink*."

Liza went over to check it out, rubbing it thoughtfully between her thumb and index finger. Epic nastiness, I know.

"It's definitely some kind of soy ink," she said, sniffing the freshly stained tips of her fingers. "Like the kind they use for newspapers."

"You think it's a clue?" Carter asked hopefully.

Liza shook her head. "I don't know. Could be. Let's keep looking."

And not ten seconds later, I heard, "Ooh! Found something!"

Yep. It was Carter. *Again*. Man, he must've been Sherlock's long-lost, sangre-slurping cousin or something!

This time when I turned to look, I saw a dozen or so small somethings—beads, it looked like—glinting in the center of his padded palm. With a fang-toothed grin, he held them out to us.

"Way to go, Carter!" I said, clapping the big guy on the arm. "See, now *that* could be a clue!"

"Oh no!" Ernie shrieked. His eyes, huge and full of terror,

84

were locked on the beads. "It's the haunted piñata! It must've eaten someone, then spat up their necklace like an owl regurgitating the bones of its prey!"

Yeah, I might've shivered at that grotesque visual. Liza, though, only groaned. "Gimme a break already . . ." she said. She leaned forward to examine the beads more closely. "Those are anti-hex beads. The ones Ms. Blanco sells at her bodega. Some people believe they can ward off the piñata. They get super popular around here every six years or so."

"Those must've been defective then," I couldn't help pointing out.

"Ooh!" Carter scooped up another handful. "Found some more!"

"Hey, you can find just about anything in the dark, huh?" Ernie said, sounding pretty impressed.

Carter grinned proudly. "Chupacabras got real good night vision. Very sharp."

"I can see that."

"Sure, but we can see it even better."

Ernie opened his mouth like he was going to say something, but then I guess he just decided to let it go.

There was a soft crunch of grass to our left, and

I realized that Liza had wandered off, the bouncing beam of her flashlight casting wild shadows over the faraway trees.

"Liza! Carter found some more beads!" I shouted.

"I found something, too!" she shouted back.

We all hustled over, tripping on roots and fallen branches, and saw what that "something" was. Lying flat in the center of her open palm was a small, brand-new-looking matchbox. The letters BFFCU had been stamped on one side. And when she slid it open, I saw that three of the matches were missing.

CHAPTER 15

This whole haunted piñata business was getting pretty weird pretty fast. If Liza was right, that meant some evil arsonist was preying on people's superstitions and taking advantage of an old town legend to set fires and terrorize everyone. Which, if you think about it, might have been even more terrifying than a haunted piñata monster on a forty-year revenge tour. Well, maybe not *that* terrifying. But it was close.

None of us said much as we made our way home later that night, but you could practically hear the hamster wheel spinning inside Liza's brilliant cabeza. She was channeling her inner Nancy Drew and had probably come up with about a thousand different theories just in the twenty or so minutes it took us to reach her house.

But it wasn't until lunch the following day that

she finally decided to share with the rest of the class (i.e., Ernie and me).

"I think I figured it out!" she whispered, slamming a newspaper down on the lunch table with a resounding *smack!* My leaning tower of Oreo Minis teetered perilously in the aftershock.

Ernie and I had just been excitedly discussing the latest release of our favorite Star Wars comic. And apparently he thought everybody else was, too, because he said, "Yeah, so do I! Like I told Jorge, all the facts point to a crooked Republic leader, but I see the Sith's fingerprints all over it. If I had to bet, I'd say we got another Senator Palpatine situation on our hands."

"I'm not talking about Star Wars, Wookiee brain!" Liza sighed. "I'm talking about who burned down my dad's shop!"

That got me sitting up pretty fast. "Wait, what? Who was it?"

"Him!"

"That's Baron von Belcherstaub," she explained, pointing at the big hombre on the front page. "He owns that fancy bank up near Ernie's house."

"He's an actual baron," Ernie informed me.

I nodded. "I've seen him around town."

"With his 'unique' fashion sense, he's a pretty hard man to miss," Liza said. "Anyway, I spent a little while down at the local library this morning and found at least another two dozen newspaper articles with his photograph. And in every single one, he's wearing a different ridiculous suit and smoking a different brand of cigar. The man clearly has no clue about the long-term cardiovascular damage caused by tobacco use. But anyway, guess what *else* he's always got?"

"One of those silly looking hats?" I guessed.

"Well, yeah, but I'm talking about *that*!" She pointed at the baron's hand. No, wait. At the pack of matches clutched loosely between his stubby manicured fingers. Printed on the front were the letters BFFCU.

"Hey, those look just like the matches we found in the woods!" Ernie said, plucking the words right out of my brain.

Liza, of course, was all smiles. "BFFCU stands for Boca Falls Federal Credit Union. The baron's bank!"

"That's actually kind of incriminating," I had to admit. "But hold up. Just because the man carries the same kind of matches doesn't automatically make him an arsonist."

"It's true," Ernie agreed. "They hand those things out at the bank like candy. Plus, how do we even know those matches were used to start the fire in the first place?"

"We don't," Liza said. "But isn't it awfully suspicious that we happened to find a matchbox with three missing matches not twenty yards from the shop? And isn't it *equally* suspicious that we also happened to find them right where Cathy claimed to have seen the haunted piñata monster?"

At the mere mention of the haunted piñata, Ernie quickly knocked on wood (i.e., our lunch table), tossed a sprinkle of Oreo crumbs over his shoulder, and then tossed a whole Oreo into his mouth.

Meanwhile, I was just trying to play connect the dots. "So you really think this dude burned down your dad's shop?"

"Where there's smoke, there's fire, right?" Liza shrugged. "It's what my Spidey-senses are screaming."

Ernie said, "Well, then riddle me this, Peter Parker:

Why? What exactly is this guy's beef with . . . well, *beef*?"

I shook my head. "That's Batman, dude."

Ernie shook his head back. "Huh?"

" 'Riddle me this' is what the Riddler always says. It's got nothing to do with Spider-Man. He's from a totally different superhero universe."

E-dog rolled his eyes. "Whatever. My point is, what's the baron got to gain by torching the local butcher's shop?"

"You just asked the million-dollar question," Liza said with a sly grin. "Or should I say, the *multi*million-dollar question . . ."

Liza's finger tapped excitedly on the top left-hand corner of the newspaper. I skimmed the headline. It read:

THE NEXT CARNEGIE OR THE NEXT VANDERBILT? BARON VON BELCHERSTAUB'S BOLD TEN-MILLION-DOLLAR PLAN TO SPREAD ECONOMIC PROSPERITY TO EVERY CORNER OF BOCA FALLS.

"I don't get it," I admitted.

"It's simple, Jorge. *Money!* That's what Baron von Belcherstaub would get out of burning down my dad's shop. See, the baron's bank specializes in real estate development and loans. Basically, they go around buying up people's land and building things like shopping malls or railroads on it." As Liza spoke, she dug a big, laminated map of Boca Falls out of her backpack. She laid it carefully down in front of us, saying, "And my dad's shop is smack-dab in the middle of an up-and-coming part of town! In fact, it's right here between three of the baron's other development projects." With her SAVE THE DOLPHINS–embellished fingernail, she traced a circle around her pop's shop. "And the thing is, he knows my dad won't sell to him. *Ever.*"

"How does he know that?" I asked.

"Because he's already tried to buy my dad out three times and each time my dad flat-out told him to go bake a cake."

"What do pastries have to do with this?" Ernie wanted to know.

Liza ignored him. "Like I said, that shop means everything to my dad. It's the first thing he and my mom ever built together. Their first business. It's more than just some grocery store, Jorge. It's a memory of my mom. And it's a part of him. A part of *both* of us." She hesitated for a second, her voice thick, her eyes all round and shiny behind her her wide-rimmed glasses. "Not to mention the fact that I know the baron hates my dad. Once, he cut off my dad's line of credit at the bank and even tried to have him arrested when he went down there to complain."

Whoa. Okay. So there was some serious heat between those two. The sort of sneaky, "This town isn't big enough for the both of-us" type of stuff you always saw on telenovelas.

Plus, Liza's logic was pretty hard to argue against. That banker dude had what any good CSI detective would call a clear motive.

And besides, with a villain-esque name like Baron von Belcherstaub, the man had to be guilty of *something*, right?

I popped an Oreo in my mouth. "Okay, so let me get this straight: You're saying the baron's plan is basically to run your dad out of town so he can buy up his store?"

"Exactly! Think about it, Jorge . . . It had to be

somebody. It was either somebody, or it was a *haunted piñata*."

"I vote haunted piñata," Ernie said very sincerely. And when Liza shot him her fiercest narrow-eyed glare, he added, "*What?*"

Taking a sip of my Capri Sun, I weighed the facts and considered the evidence. Who was the sneaky, fire-loving villain behind the arson? Greedy banker or real-life haunted piñata monster? Hmm . . .

It was a close call, but the odds had to favor greedy banker.

"All right, I'm with you, Liza. The baron is our suspect numero uno. So what do we do now?"

"Now," she said with a mischievous grin, "we just have to prove it."

CHAPTER 16

Not surprisingly, it didn't take Liza very long to come up with a plan. And it was a pretty slick one, too. It went something like this: First, we'd show up at the baron's bank after school and demand to speak with him. Then, once we got him alone in his office, we'd pretend that we knew everything—like we'd unraveled his entire scheme!—and hopefully sucker a confession out of him. A confession Liza planned to capture in glorious HD via a phone cleverly concealed in her bookbag.

E-dog, however, brought up a smart point: "In order to pull that off, we're going to need some serious muscle," he said.

Liza frowned. "What are you talking about?"

"Duh! We'll need some backup in case von Belcherstaub really *is* a psycho arsonist and decides to eliminate the only three people in the last forty years to find him out!"

Like I said, a smart point.

His idea about *whose* muscles he wanted to recruit, though, was—well, not so smart.

I said skeptically, "Dude, one silly collar is *not* going to be able to hide what Carter really is!"

With a sly, confident look, Ernie said, "Oh, yeah? Ever heard of Clark Kent?"

Liza reluctantly shrugged. "He's not wrong."

In the end, we decided that we didn't really have a choice. We were definitely going to need some backup on this one. And I'm not going to lie: I was pretty amped about springing our little hidden camera surprise on the baron. He sounded like the kind of jerk that up-and-coming jerks study under and receive diplomas from.

But later that day, when the four of us actually arrived at the Boca Falls Credit Union, *we* were the ones who were in for a surprise.

Ernie said, "Is it me or did our plan just go up in flames?"

It wasn't just him.

A moment later, some little kid on a bike pulled in front of us. He was sipping greedily on a Big Gulp and looking Carter up and

down. "*Geesh!* That's one ugly pooch you got there!" he said. "What's his name?"

"Ugly," I answered dryly.

The kid looked surprised. "Really?"

"Ironic, huh?"

Carter, who already wasn't exactly thrilled with having to play a pooch for the day, began to growl. Then—

Sensing he wasn't making any friends, the kid stammered, "S-s-see you guys later!" and he pedaled off like an entire army of howling Dementors was after him.

Liza, meanwhile, was trying to get some dude's attention—a tall, pudgy, bald hombre with the chewed-down stub of a yellow pencil stuck behind one ear, holding a notepad. She went up beside him, tapping him on the shoulder of his tan sports coat. "Excuse me, Mr. Rathbone, what happened here?!"

Oh, duh! That was Raymond Rathbone, the owner of the largest local newspaper, the *Boca Tribune*. Guess his press badge and reporter's pad should've probably tipped me off.

Mr. Rathbone whirled to face her. "*A FIRE!*" he cried hysterically. "*A TERRIBLE FIRE!*"

Frowning, Liza shook her head. "When did it start?!"

"Early this morning! Around six a.m. That's all I was able to get out of the fire chief."

Liza's shocked eyes instantly found mine. I knew what she was thinking, because it was exactly what I was thinking: 6:00 a.m. was right about the same time that *her* dad's shop had caught fire the day before! Talk about a creepy coincidence. And maybe even creepier: a pattern was now beginning to emerge . . .

Off to our right, two firefighters in matching blue

T-shirts and orange suspenders were standing at the back end of a fire truck, talking loudly.

"The chief told me the fire started in the vault," one said.

"Impossible," answered the other. "It was locked. Nobody could've gotten in there."

Then the first one said, "Yeah, nobody except a *haunted piñata*."

They both shivered.

"¿Oíste eso?" whispered Carter, nudging my side. "You heard dem?"

A few curious eyes swiveled in his direction. And unfortunately, they weren't just Ernie's.

I resisted the urge to glare at the bigmouthed mosquito. I didn't think it would be wise to draw any more attention in his direction. Instead I just kept staring straight ahead and growled out of the corner of my mouth, "Uh-huh. But dogs don't talk, remember? And they don't nudge, either, so maintain all four paws on the ground, will ya?!"

A second later, I noticed that Liza was staring curiously across the shopping center at some lanky lady who was reclining coolly against a shiny white pickup. The words CITY ENGINEER'S OFFICE were emblazoned across the side doors.

"What's up?" I asked Liza.

She shook her head, still staring at the lady. "I feel like I've seen her before, but I can't remember where."

I shrugged. I couldn't really help her there. I was terrible with remembering faces.

Straight ahead, a squat, heavyset dude in a canary-yellow suit and bowler hat was pushing his way rudely through the crowd toward us.

Baron von Belcherstaub. You couldn't have missed him even with both eyes closed.

As if his awful taste in clothes didn't already make him stick out like the world's sorest thumb, the baron was acting like a tantrum-throwing toddler—stomping his feet and clenching his fists and basically just crying and whining at some other dude in a striped firefighter's jacket, helmet, and high black boots, who, if he wasn't a firefighter, clearly liked to dress like one.

"Fire chief, listen to me!" pleaded the baron. "My finest cigars are in there! Please just let me run in and rescue them!"

"Mr. von Belcherstaub," replied the fire chief calmly, "as I have already explained, it would be against civil ordinance for me to let you enter that building—especially while it's still in the process of *burning down*! I'll say it again: no one is, or will be, allowed inside until the fire's been put out and we can ascertain the safety of the structure."

"But my cigars!" bellowed the baron, his big eyes bulging. "They were Cubans! Did you hear me? CU-BANS!"

"Mr. von Belcherstaub, I don't care if they were from Mars, you *aren't* getting in there!"

The fire chief had the baron by his meaty upper

arm and was guiding him, not so gently, in our direc-tion, away from the fire. "Mr. von Belcherstaub, I'm going to have to ask you to remain right here, please."

The baron's desperate eyes swept wildly around, as if searching for some judge or jury to plead his case to. They found Liza's.

"This is unthinkable!" he shouted. "UNTHINK-ABLE! First, your father's shop. Now *my* bank! I—I know I haven't always seen eye to eye with your papa, but I've already ordered my finance officers to assist him with any and all expenses his insurance doesn't cover. He *must* rebuild! We MUST stand together as a community! Every single one of us!" He paused as a shadow of fear darkened his pale and blotchy features. "And now more than ever. For a dreadful curse lies upon this town, and the piñata's wrath has once again awakened! I fear that if we do not fight together, we will all burn alone!"

CHAPTER 17

"So much for the banker theory, huh?" I said as we made our way back through the woods a little later.

"Unless he burned down the bank to throw us off his scent," Liza hypothesized.

Which, of course, was a possibility. But I wasn't buying it. "That's a bit over the top, no? Plus, I don't think he would have gone as far as sacrificing his precious

Verdict (surprisingly): not guilty.

cigars. They were Cubans, didn't you hear him?"

"Well, if it's not the baron, then it's somebody else. There's an arsonist running around Boca Falls, and it's up to *us* to smoke him out."

"There *is* no arsonist!" Ernie suddenly snapped. "Wake up and smell the salami! It's the haunted piñata! You heard the baron!" Then, in his best Baron von Belcherstaub impersonation: "The town has a *terrible* curse upon it! We will burn! We will all burn!"

Liza zapped him with her trademark eye roll. "I'll believe in cursed, fire-breathing piñatas when I see one."

"Yeah, except by then it'll be too late!"

Just then, another possibility struck me. It was a wild one—no doubt. But a possibility all the same. "Hey, what do you think about Zane and his knuckle-dragging goons?"

"I try not to," said Ernie. "My doctor told me that it's bad for my blood pressure."

"I mean in terms of them being the arsonists. Maybe they're the ones behind this latest round of fires! You know—the whole copycat thing you were talking about," I said to Liza.

Liza considered that. "Possible," she said after a moment. "But not likely. Stuff like arson usually takes a bit of planning, and Zane and his bunch of soccer hooligans probably couldn't muster up a single brain cell between the entire *team*."

She had a point.

"Anybody else smell dat?" asked Carter, sniffing lightly at the air. "Smells like . . . chicharrones. And Cherry Coke."

I couldn't help but lol at that. The dude's stomach was like the local IHOP: open for business 24-7.

"You dream about fried pork rinds, don't you?" I teased.

Carter grinned. "I not dreaming, Jorge. I really smell chi—"

BOOM!

An ear-busting sound rocked the world. Everybody froze.

I shouted, "*What was*—?"

But no sooner had the words flown out of my mouth than there was another earth-shattering *BOOM!*

And this time, something bounced off a nearby tree and the tree erupted in a burst of bark and splinters.

I saw Liza's eyes widen with sudden understanding.

But before I could ask her what the heck was going on, she screamed, "*RUN!*"

No one really argued.

We ran.

Dead leaves and twigs crunched under our sneakers as we plunged headlong into the trees.

Rocks and roots snatched at my feet. Branches swiped at my face.

Another *BOOM!*

Too close.

Waaay too close!

And next thing I knew, one of Carter's strong, furry arms was wrapping around my waist from behind, dragging me to the ground even as a giant geyser of dirt sprayed straight up into the air just ahead of us, and the world shook and leaves rained down like green confetti.

We hit the ground in a tangle of arms and legs. Which, by the way, also included Liza's and Ernie's arms and legs, because Carter had apparently tackled all of us at the same time.

Panicking, rolling for cover behind a nearby boulder, I screamed, "WHAT IS HAPPENING?!"

I mean, *seriously*! I was having flashbacks to one of those old black-and-white war movies you sometimes run across while channel surfing!

Ernie shrieked, "THE PIÑATA MONSTER! IT'S COMING FOR US!"

"It's not the piñata, halibut brain!" Liza shouted. "Someone's throwing *bombs* at us!"

"UN BIG GAME HUNTER!" screamed Carter, burying his face in the grass. "SKENNYRD'S BACK!"

Then from somewhere in the trees came, "KEEP YOUR HEADS DOWN, KIDDOS! I'LL BLOW THAT THING TO SMITHEREENS!"

Another *BOOM!* Then the log Carter was hiding behind EXPLODED into—well, smithereens! Chunks of fuzzy green moss and dirty brown woodchips pelted us.

And that was when it finally dawned on me:

Whoever was chucking the bombs wasn't chucking them at *us*.

They were chucking them at *Carter*!

CHAPTER 18

You know how people say that true friendship is sacrificial? Meaning, you'd give up your own life to save your buddy's?

Well, I guess I must've really been a true friend then, because the first thing that popped into my head was to jump to my feet and start waving my arms in big, stupid X's, trying to draw the mad bomber's attention. Which was exactly what I did.

"HEY, ¡PARA!" I screamed at the top of my lungs. "STOP! STOP IT, YO!"

Just then, maybe fifty yards away, a clump of shrubs and weedy grass stood up. Stood right up like a person!

Then I realized that it WAS a person!

I instantly recognized him, too.

His name was Red Wilson. He was an ex-Marine who lived out here in the middle of the woods somewhere, and who everyone in town pretty much avoided for one reason or another. Guess I could see why.

"STOP LOBBING BOMBS AT US!" I screamed, still waving my arms. "THAT'S MY—" I nearly said *chupacabra*, but I was pretty sure that would've only made things worse. "MY DOG!"

"It is?!" cried Red. Honestly, if I'd grown a pair of wings, flown way up into the sky, and pooped all over this dude's head, I don't think he would've looked any more surprised.

"Yes, all right?! *Geez!* Now put the dynamite away before you blow somebody up!"

I elbowed him in the ribs. Hard. "He means mastiff," I told Red.

Bathrobe Rambo considered that. "Half Doberman, half mastiff, huh? Well, it's one hundred percent *ugly,* if you don't mind my saying so!"

I didn't. Carter, on the other hand, began to growl. Something told me he wasn't Red's biggest fan.

"Easy, boy . . . *easy,*" I said, rubbing behind Carter's ears. I'm pretty sure he wasn't a fan of that, either.

Red, meanwhile, was staring down at Carter as if he'd just hatched from a chicken egg. "But wasn't it walking on two legs just now?"

"Oh, ha! Right!" I frantically searched my brain for a half-decent excuse. There didn't seem to be one in there, so I went with, "That's because I, uh, taught him a new trick! How to walk on his hind legs. He was just practicing."

Total weak sauce, I know. But Red seemed to be buying it, because he was looking mighty embarrassed all of a sudden.

"Well, my gosh, kids, I'm so sorry! I honestly thought that thing was *stalking* you! I saw it coming up behind y'all, real sneaky-like, and, well—I guess I panicked."

Ha! Talk about the understatement of the century.

"That can happen," I said. "We appreciate the concern, though."

"Yeah, just not the trying-to-blow-us-to-bits part," Ernie put in. "By the way, is that *real* dynamite?"

Mr. Boom Boom Sticks shook his head. "No, just a few homemade poppers taped together. I used to be in the fireworks business." And now he hung his head in shame. "But I guess it's true what they say, eh? Your nerves are the first thing to go when you get to be my age. And all this talk about the haunted piñata being back ain't helpin' mine any." He rubbed his scruffy chin distractedly. "The whole town's coming apart, you know. And I'm afraid it's only a matter of time before that thing strikes again."

"Mr. Wilson, you don't actually *believe* in the legend, do you?" I asked uneasily.

He gave a sort of helpless shrug. With all the bits and pieces of vegetation dangling off him, the dude looked like a really depressed oak tree. "Truthfully? I've never been one for fairy tales. But it's hard to argue when you've seen what I have."

"What do you mean?" asked Carter.

Yep. *Carter.*

The sangre-slurping cryptid who was *supposed* to be pretending to be a dog.

That guy.

I squeezed my eyes shut. Guess the cat was officially out of the bag, huh? Or the *chupacabra*, anyway.

I could practically hear Red's eyes widening like saucers in his leathery, camouflage-paint-streaked face. "DID THAT DOG JUST TALK?!"

CHAPTER 19

"Talk? Ha! You mean, *bark*?!" Liza jumped in. (Hooray for Liza!) "He has an *extremely* unique bark, doesn't he?"

"Oh, yes!" I quickly agreed. "The unique-est! Though sometimes it really does sound like they're trying to talk to us in their own special way, doesn't it? Our pets, I mean."

Yeah, I was pouring it on. And maybe a little *too* thickly. But at least it seemed to be working.

Red was sort of nodding along now, his eyes slightly glazed, looking a little dizzy. "Guess so. And I guess it's your hearing that goes after your nerves do, eh?"

We all just agreed with him, Carter even joining the bobblehead gang until I smacked him on the side.

Then, after a few moments, Liza said, "Mr.

Wilson, what did you mean by what you said before? About what you'd seen?"

The ex-military man's bony shoulders went up and down. "You have to keep in mind that I've lived in Boca Falls for almost thirty years now. Right here in these woods. I was even a local firefighter at one time. Deputy to the chief. I've been around el bloque, as they say."

"You were a firefighter?" I asked, surprised.

"As a matter of fact, 'bout twelve years ago, I was in charge of investigating the string of mysterious green fires. And the thing is, every six years, like demonic clockwork, they always start up again. The legends become whispers, and the whispers begin to fill every ear in town until everyone's thinking about that old Blackbriar curse." His voice had dropped to a hoarse pitch and a shadow of fear now darkened his features. "I don't want to believe in some candy-stuffed, fire-breathin' monster, but it's hard to totally dismiss the possibility when you've seen all those smoking buildings and all those broken hearts."

"So you never figured out what was going on with the fires?" I asked.

Red shook his head gloomily. "No, unfortunately,

I did not. I did get *fired*, though. The chief forced me out. Someone had to pay the piper for the lack of answers, and I guess I was the logical scapegoat, leading the investigation and all." His gaze shifted to Liza. "By the way, I'm sorry about your dad's shop. That man cut the best brisket in three counties. I hate to see bad things happen to good people. But you tell your daddy I'll be the first in line soon as he opens up again."

Liza smiled. "I'll tell him, Mr. Wilson. Thanks."

Bathrobe Rambo's eyes had gone glassy, and he stared off into the woods as if lost in his own little firework-chucking world. "Anyway, I haven't even seen the scariest stuff. You've got people in town that have actually come face-to-face with that demon. Or at least they claim they have."

"*Face-to-face?*" Carter gasped, and I quickly reached a hand behind me to clamp his mouth shut once and for all. If only Ernie's dog collar had come with a *muzzle* attachment . . .

Red, for his part, just stood there blinking down at the chupacabra like he wasn't even sure which way was up anymore. Finally, he shrugged and said, "Yep, nariz-a-nariz, as they say."

"Like who?" I asked. "Who's come nose-to-nose with it?"

"Oh, plenty of people. Ms. Blanco, for one. I'm sure you all know Ms. Blanco. She owns the little bodega up on Main Street? Come to think of it, you might want to have a talk with her," he said, turning to Liza. "She might've seen something the night your dad's shop burned down."

Liza was shaking her head. "What do you mean, 'she might've seen something'?"

"Well, a couple of days ago, I saw her walking east through these very woods. And about a twenty-minute stroll in that direction would've put her only a stone's throw from your daddy's shop at right around the time of the fire."

And I'm sure you could've guessed our reactions...

The beads!

The ones we'd found in the woods!

Those must've been *Ms. Blanco's* beads!

The silence that followed was so thick you could've sliced and diced it, deep-fried it, and served it with a side of arroz rojo.

A moment later Liza managed, "You—you're sure you saw her walking that way?"

"Pretty sure," replied Mr. Wilson. "I couldn't swear it was her or anything; it was kinda dark out. But I saw a mess of beaded necklaces and bracelets glinting in the moonlight. She might've been walking her dog by here. She's done that for years."

The four of us were all still blinking around at each other in OMG shock when Red snapped off a crisp military salute and said, "Anywho, you kids shouldn't be walking through the woods alone. Not with the way things are at the moment." Then he jerked a dirt-smudged thumb over his shoulder. "By the way, I got a couple extra bags of fried pork rinds and a few cans of Cherry Coke in the cooler, if any of you are interested."

"Tol' you I smelled chicharrones!" Carter shouted.

CHAPTER 20

It was almost a two-mile trek from Red's double-wide in the woods to the little bodega on Main Street, and the whole way over Carter didn't stop scratching and Ernie didn't stop yapping. Carter's issue: he'd picked up a few unfriendly "passengers" (aka, fleas) while going all Dwayne "The Rock" Johnson in the woods dodging firecrackers. Ernie's deal: based on the beads we'd found and the eyewitness report placing Ms. Blanco near the butcher shop at the time of the fire, he was now absolutely, positively, slap-handcuffs-on-the-woman convinced that our friendly neighborhood bodega owner was, in fact, a not-so-friendly homicidal homegrown arsonist.

Liza and I, on the other hand, were still trying to abide by that whole "innocent until proven guilty" thing. But let me tell you, the weight of evidence was making it tough!

As we strolled in, a familiar electronic *ding-dong* greeted us, and the sweet, smiling face of Ms. Blanco looked up from the cash register.

Ms. Blanco was one of the most beloved people in town. Her shop was almost always full, and she had nothing but five-star reviews on Yelp. Well, besides the single three-star review that Paz stuck in there just because she was like that.

We all said hello. Yep, including Carter. But thankfully Ms. B. didn't catch that. She said, "Like the sign on the window says, I don't mind dogs in here; but that's one strange-looking Chihuahua!"

"Oh, he's not a Chihuahua," I said. "He's a Chihuacabra. It's a brand-new breed."

Ms. Blanco looked like she'd just seen Dr. Strange's flying cape flutter past her window, then pointed back over our heads. "Bueno, the candy is in aisle five. The ice cream's in the freezer. Oh, and I just got a delicious new flavor in the slushy machine—super mango berry blast!"

Carter's eyes lit up. He and Ernie quickly followed their growling stomachs toward the brightly colored slushy machine in the middle of the store. Liza had to yank them both back.

"All right, all right," Ernie grumbled, straightening his shirt. "But let's make this quick. I've never tried super mango berry blast before, and it sounds *epic*!"

Suddenly, a real hard-edged look came into E-dog's eyes (kind of like those tough courtroom lawyers on TV shows), and he said—well, more like *growled*—"Ms. Blanco, where were you on the morning of of Monday, November sixth, when the local butcher shop was burned down? And more importantly, can you *prove* it?"

There's this face my grandpa makes when he gets a really bad case of gas. That was pretty much the face Ms. B. was making now. "¿Perdón?" she said.

"This isn't *CSI: Miami*, Ernie!" Liza hissed into his ear. "Let *me* do the talking." Then, turning back to everyone's favorite bodega owner, she smiled and said, "We're sorry to bother you, Ms. Blanco. But we were just wondering if you had seen anything odd over the past couple of days or so."

"Odd?" Ms. B. shook her head, and her many necklaces jingled like the percussion section of an orchestra. "I'd say things in general right now are pretty odd, what with the fires and all. But I haven't seen anything that I would personally classify as odd. Why do you ask?"

"Red Wilson mentioned that he thought he had seen you walking through the woods the day before yesterday, at about the time my dad's shop caught fire; so we were curious if you happened to see anyone or anything strange in the area."

Just then, I saw the weird-looking dude standing at the far end of the counter slip a sneaky little peek in our direction. It wasn't much, just a tiny flick of the eyes. But when he realized I'd caught him, his attention dropped right back to the glossy magazine in his hands as if it contained the winning lottery numbers.

"I wish I could help," said Ms. B. with a little shrug. "But I'm afraid Red is mistaken. I wasn't out that morning at all. I was home. In fact, at about the time the newspaper said your daddy's shop caught fire, I was pounding on my neighbor's door because my power had gone out and that triggered my alarm system."

The Gru look-alike who was pretend-reading the mag tossed another sneaky look in our direction. And this time, he decided to toss over some words, too.

"She's not lying," he said, with a grin that could've curdled milk. "Though I wish she was, because someone hammering on your door at six in the morning isn't the most pleasant wakeup call in the world."

I bet.

The front of his work shirt, I noticed, read LINUS LESTER over one pocket and SECURITY AND LOCKSMITH-ING over the other. My finely honed detective instincts told me he must be the local locksmith. Yep, Jorge Lopez, master sleuth, at your service.

"So . . . Ms. Blanco was knocking on your door at

the time of the fire?" asked Liza, sounding a little off balance. Like maybe she hadn't expected that. Like maybe she'd been expecting an open-and-shut case against Ms. B.

"That's an affirmative," said the creepy dude with another creepy grin. The mouthful of chompers this guy was so quick to flash would've made nine out of ten dentists consider permanent retirement. Man, had he never heard of the Colgate company?

Ms. Bodega, meanwhile, perched on the edge of her tall stool, watched us for a moment. Then a secret smile began to spread slowly across her face. It was the kind of smile that would've made a polar bear want to put on a winter coat.

"Ah, I think know what you three *really* want to know," she practically purred. "You want to know if I saw *la piñata* . . . You three aren't afraid of it, *are you*?"

"Yes!" Ernie gulped. "Very afraid, ma'am!"

"Why would we be afraid of it?" Liza said defiantly. "It's just a silly legend kept alive by children and wild superstitions."

"Ah, that's what I believed, too, when I first moved into town," said the bodega owner, her eyes darkening ominously. "But the tale is told by more than children, my dears. In fact, I *myself* have seen the monster!"

And all of a sudden, it was Ernie who looked like he'd seen a monster. Every bit of color had drained from the kid's face, and when he spoke, his voice climbed so high on the octave ladder that it made Alvin the Chipmunk sound like Darth Vader. "Y-you have?"

"Sí," murmured Ms. Blanco, "I have. And even more terrifying, it saw *me*!"

I cleared my throat, trying to keep my voice from out-squeaking Ernie's as I said, "Uh, when was this?"

"Some years ago. Six, to be exact. And almost to *the day*. It was during the monster's last reign of terror that I found myself walking in the woods near Mr. Wilson's property. I was taking Priscilla, my darling Chihuahua, out for a stroll as I so often used to do, and it was quite late at night. I had just come to the end of my usual route when I heard a strange stirring in the trees. At first, I assumed it was simply some forest critter. A fox, perhaps. But as I turned and my eyes slowly penetrated the gloom, I saw it . . . the most terrifying sight these old eyes have *ever* seen!"

Suddenly Ms. Blanco leapt up onto the counter

like a pouncing cat, flapping her arms wildly as she shouted, "A living NIGHTMARE! A creature as black as death, with a face wreathed by ash and hellfire!" Her voice was eager but full of dread, as if she was afraid her words could somehow hocus-pocus the monster into existence. "I saw it, children! There, looming in the darkness—*the haunted piñata!*"

"W-what did it look like?" Carter asked uneasily.

Ms. B.—probably assuming that one of us non-bloodsuckers had asked it—snapped her gray eyes to me and said, "Its shape is that of a typical piñata—donkey-like, squat. But do not be fooled! That creature is no more papier-mâché than you or I! It is an abomination! A fire-breathing *HORROR!*"

"So what'd you do?!" Ernie squeaked.

"What *could* I do?" snapped the bodega owner. "I stood as one dead! Held up only by my failing grip on Priscilla's leash, while my precious little princess barked and barked, trying to protect her mama. Trying to frighten the monstruo away! But the monster would not be frightened.

"It watched me, hungrily, in silence. Then its eyes, which at first appeared lifeless—like a doll's eyes— suddenly blazed to life! A flaming poison-green, they

were! And they looked *straight* at me . . . into my very *soul*! It was in that moment that I experienced true fear. An awful blood-freezing fear, which rendered me unable to move, think, or even scream! Oh, and how desperately I wanted to scream! But my tongue was a prisoner in the presence of that evil!

"Then, somehow—I cannot explain how—my legs found strength even while the rest of me melted in terror. I turned and fled into the darkness, and the monster pursued. Its shrieking cries filled the woods, and it was gaining on me, second after second. I could feel its boiling, stinking breath singeing the nape of my neck as it bore down upon me!"

"But as I learned that night," said Ms. B., "from monsters like those, there is no escape. Soon I found myself hemmed in, as if by the night itself, with my back pressed against the trunk of a dead oak and my heart hammering in my throat even as the wretched thing's flaming eyes burned in the cold night air."

"And then what?" screeched Ernie, squeezing my arm so hard I was pretty sure he'd left permanent finger tattoos on my skin. "What'd you do?!"

"The only thing I could!" exclaimed Ms. Bodega. "I threw up my hands, trying to shield my face from the piñata monster's terrible gaze. And suddenly, an instant before it could incinerate me with a blast of its fiery breath, the demon froze!"

"IT FROZE?" we all gasped in unison.

Yeah, that was just about the last thing I'd expected to hear.

"Sí, it *froze!*" said Ms. B.

"B-but, why?" Ernie wanted to know.

"Ah, I asked myself the very same question at the time. And eventually, I discovered the answer. It froze because of my *beads!*"

Her beads? I paused to let that sink in. Only it didn't sink very far. It just sort of floated there, like a dead fish, on the surface of my brain. "You mean a fire-breathing, undead piñata monster was scared away by some plastic wrist ornaments?"

"Yes, ¡exactamente!" Ms. B. held her bejeweled arms proudly out toward us. The mess of colorful bracelets jingled and jangled like Santa's famous sleigh. "I'll be completely honest with you: I'm not sure what it is about the beads exactly. But there must be something the piñata fears about the material, or the colors, or perhaps even the sound! It is the only form of protection I trust with my life, which is why it is the *only* protection that I sell."

She slumped back down on her stool, as if that terrifying trip down memory lane had taken a lot out of her, and her voice grew even more ominous somehow. "You might think me a senile old woman," she said, "a peddler of old stories and cheap trinkets; but everything I have told you is the absolute *truth*. The fire of an unquenchable evil has once again been stoked in Boca Falls. The charred scent of its presence already chokes the air. But to revisit your original question: Ever since that day, I never walk through the woods at night. For I know all too well the horror that lurks in this town . . ."

CHAPTER 21

"But what about the beads we found in the woods?" Ernie managed between mouthfuls of super mango berry blast. "And what Red said? Someone was out there. But, who?"

The question to end all questions, I thought.

"That's going to be next to impossible to figure out," Liza grumbled, even while she slurped on her slushy. "Ms. Blanco's beads are super popular around here, which means it could've been practically anybody."

She was right. The beads weren't going to help narrow down our suspects list, like, *at all.* And to be honest, after story time with Ms. B., and seeing the fear of that encounter still fresh in her eyes (not to mention the million and one beads jingling and jangling from her wrists and neck), I couldn't help but wonder if maybe the legend was . . . more than just a legend. If maybe it *wasn't* a local loco starting the fires. If maybe some fire-breathing piñata monstruo really *was* haunting our sleepy little town. It was wild to consider, I know. I mean, haunted piñata monsters should probably top anyone's top ten list of Things That Don't Actually Exist.

But then again, so should chupacabras, and I just

so happened to be best friends with one.

All of a sudden, Count Dracula's significantly taller, significantly *hairier* cousin cried, "Ayayaya!" and we all spun around to face him.

"What is it?" I asked Carter. "You figured something out?"

He gave me a big, sheepish, sideways grin. "Sí. If you drink dis stuff too fast, you brain freezes."

Great. A chupacabra comedian. Just what this town needs.

Beside me, looking pretty worried, Ernie said, "I don't know . . . I'm back on team haunted piñata. That's my suspect numero uno again."

Liza glared at him. "Seriously? Your prime suspect is a haunted, candy-stuffed donkey?"

Ernie shrugged. "Well, who do *you* think is more likely behind the fires?"

"Literally *anyone* else!" she snapped.

Halfway to Liza's house, her phone started playing a catchy Selena Gomez song as a ringtone. It was her dad. They talked for about a minute before Liza said, "I'm almost there," and hung up.

I'd seen popped balloons that looked less deflated than she did, so I said, "What's up? What happened?"

Liza shrugged, all gloomy-like, and kicked a rock down the dusty shoulder of the road. "Nothing. My dad just wants to show me a few of the houses he's been looking at."

"Houses?"

"Yeah, he wants to move east."

"Oh, so closer to Jorge's grandparents?" asked Ernie. "That's cool."

"No, I don't mean East Boca Falls. I mean East Coast. As in, Augusta, Georgia."

I gaped. "Why is he looking at houses in *Georgia*? That's, like, waaay outside our school district. It's practically on the other side of the country!"

"It *is* on the other side of the country. *Factually*, not just practically," Liza pointed out. "But my dad doesn't think it's far enough. He's thinking about Florida, too." She lifted her shoulders and then let them drop back down again with a groan. The cheer in her voice was approaching thundercloud levels. "The truth is, after the fire, he's just about had it with Boca Falls, Jorge. He wants to get out of here. For good."

CHAPTER 22

The idea of Liza packing up and hitching a ride on the U-Haul Express hit me like a Canelo Álvarez uppercut to the gut. And as if that wasn't bad enough, apparently Liza's dad wasn't the only one thinking about skipping town. According to Ernie, his parents were thinking of moving, too. In fact, they were already talking about relocating to Michigan near some extended family, in case things got any worse around here.

I could feel that awful and familiar sense of loneliness beginning to creep over me. Heck, I guess you could call it my superpower. My very own kind of Spidey-senses. I could literally *feel* when people were getting ready to leave me.

Probably because I had so much experience with it.

Honestly, it was like I'd slipped into some recurring nightmare. Here I was, starting to feel settled for the first time in my whole life. Starting to feel like I belonged. Like I had a real home, with real friends. Friends I could talk to. Friends that actually cared about me. And now that was all about to be taken away. Just like that. Just because some monster or (way more likely) some selfish prankster got a sick kick out of terrorizing an entire town.

I mean, assuming it *was* a person and not some supernatural entity we were dealing with, what was their deal? Why had they been running this haunted piñata gag for *forty years*? What joy could they possibly get out of messing with a bunch of hardworking, everyday people? Out of scaring them? Out of destroying their lives and livelihoods?

The funny part was, the more I thought about it, the more my mind kept boomeranging back to one absurd—yet absurdly *troubling*—possibility. Zane and company.

I could *so* see that bunch of bozos holding "the smoking match" on this one. It just seemed like such a bully thing to do. And I couldn't help thinking back to that day in the cafeteria when they'd set that lunch tray on fire and Zane had issued his not-so-subtle warning:

"This time it was just a lunch tray. But next time it might be your locker that catches fire. Or Madame Cureall's latest science project."

The fact was, I knew they had the mean in them to do it. But did they have the brains not to have gotten themselves caught by now?

That, I wasn't so sure about.

My theory had other problems, too. Let's say it really *was* Zane and his crew. Well, then what about all the previous fires? The ones from, like, *thirty years* ago? That obviously hadn't been them. So was it just a copycat thing? Every six years some other wannabe arsonist taking the "flaming baton" and running with it?

It was possible, I guess.

Yeah, this was an enigma on the level of Edward Nygma (that's the Riddler, for those of you who might not be DC comic buffs). I mean, where was Batman when you needed him?

To make things even worse, I was missing my mom like *crazy*. This was the longest I'd ever been away from her—away from L.A., too—and it just felt like this huge part of me was missing. Like somebody had taken one of Red's high-powered dynamite sticks and blown a great big gaping hole through the center of my chest. A hole that no amount of junk food or video games could seem to fill. I'm not saying everything back home had been all sunflowers and rainbows. It hadn't. As a matter of fact, my mom and I had never really had an easy time. We never seemed to have enough money or catch enough breaks, and we were always arguing about the silliest things. How I wore my ball cap, for instance.

Still . . . we always had each other. And when you don't have a lot of things, you quickly realize that *each other* is all you really need.

Jorge, I gotta talk to you about something. It's pretty serious.

I didn't like that sound of that. My life already had enough serious at the moment. "What's up?" I said.

"Can I tell you a quick story?"

"Huh?"

"It's an old story, but it's good. Can I tell it to you?"

"Uh, yeah. Sure. Go for it."

"It's a story about a boy," Carter began slowly, "a boy who wished he'd been born a wild animal."

"Sounds interesting so far . . ."

"This chamaco loved to spend all his free time out in the woods, playing 'round the trees and streams. And one day, he met the wildest creature of all—a chupacabra. Together, they played and they laughed and they had a real good time, you know?"

"I think I can relate a little," I said with a grin.

"But then, one mornin', when the boy woke up in his bed, he saw a fur-covered arm next to him. Then he realized it was *his* fur-covered arm! 'Cause the boy had turn into a chupacabra! No one could explain how dis happened. But from dat day, his mother had no choice but to banish him into the woods 'cause she was scared the villagers would kill him if dey saw him. And no matter how bad the boy wanted to be human again, he was forced to live the rest of his days as a chupacabra."

I tossed a handful of buttery popcorn into my mouth. "Not a bad story," I said between chews. "There's probably a life lesson in there somewhere. Could have used a bit more plot, though."

Carter said, "But it's not jess a story, Jorge. It *actually* happened."

"What are you talking about? How could that have actually happened?"

Now a very serious look came over the chupacabra's long furry face as he said, "'Cause that boy was *me*, Jorge."

Wait up.

Somebody hit rewind!

"Whoa, whoa—hold the arroz con pollo!" I shouted. "You're saying that the boy from the story—the boy who turned into a chupacabra—was . . . *you*?"

Carter nodded, a tiny, embarrassed movement.

"I—I don't get it," I stammered as my heart began tap-dancing against my rib cage.

"Didn't you listen to the story, Jorge? I was once a

boy. A regular, *human* boy—just like you! But I met a chupacabra and ..."

His words trailed slowly off as the full and terrifying meaning of what he was trying to say hit me like a runaway train. "But what—I mean, *why*—I mean, *how is that even POSSIBLE?*"

Carter wouldn't even look at me now. "It's like I jess tol' you," he whispered, staring into the faraway trees. "I started hanging out with this chupacabra I met. You know, sharing snacks and stuff. And I guess ... I guess chupacabra-ness is ... *contagious.*"

"CONTAGIOUS?!" I shrieked, almost leaping to my feet. "You mean like some kind of zombie plague?!"

He gave another small shrug. "Pretty much."

My jaw dropped and the world seemed to tilt underneath me.

O. M. G!

I mean, this couldn't be true. This was ... it was *UNTHINKABLE!* Heck, I'd been hanging out with Carter for more than two weeks! A *lot* more! And so had Liza and Ernie—

Oh my gosh—Liza and Ernie!

What was I going to tell them? What *could* I tell them?!

They were going to say it was all my fault! That I'd introduced them to Carter, that I'd brought this giant, hairy, *contagious* bloodsucker into their lives— into their homes!—and they'd be one million percent right!

But that wasn't even the worst part. No, the worst part was that soon all three of us would be forced to spend the rest of our lives in the forest!

In the woods! Like wild animals!

We would live out the rest of our days afraid, hunted, always on the move.

And always thirsting for *bloo*—

Suddenly, patient zero over here threw back his giant head and burst out laughing like a hyena who had just sucked down an entire tank of laughing gas.

"Oh man, you should see your *face* right now, Jorge!" he cried, spraying me in the face with bits of chewed-up popcorn. "¡Ay, Dios! It's too funny! Stop it, Jorge, you killin' me! You *killin'* me!"

"Dude, what are you *laughing* at?!" I snapped, flinging popcorn at him. "This ain't no laughing matter!"

"Yeah, it is! 'Cause I was jess messin' wit' you, bro! Ahahahahaha!"

Just messing with me?

He was JUST MESSING with me?

"Carter, that was *not* funny! How could you make something like that up?!"

"I jess wanted to cheer you up," he said, grinning from batty ear to ear.

"How was that supposed to cheer me up?!" I shouted at him.

"'Cause now you don't gotta be afraid of turning into a chupacabra. Duh!"

Eh. I guess could see how that might make sense in Carter's mind.

But geez.

My heart was still racing like a car at the Indy 500 as I let out a HUGE sigh of relief . . . and—well, I actually *did* start to feel a little better.

Guess the giant bloodsucker might've had a point after all.

CHAPTER 23

Early the next morning (I'm talking *cock-a-doodle-doo* early), my abuela burst into my room, going all rock 'n' roll drummer on a copper cazuela and yelling at me to get up and get dressed.

At first, in my half-asleep state, I thought she might've been getting ready to skip town (like everybody else, apparently).

But I should've known better.

Paz wasn't the type to run away. She was the type doing the chasing.

What had actually happened was that my grandpa got hired to do a little cleanup/handyman work over at Liza's dad's shop and needed my help. Obviously I didn't have a choice.

Trust me, I double-checked.

Anyway, my grandpa promised to pay me twenty smackaroos for helping him out, so I got up, changed, wolfed down a couple of Frosted Raspberry Pop-Tarts, and jumped into the shotgun seat of his beat-up old pickup.

The whole drive over, I was busy doing mental gymnastics. Trying to think through and connect the mysterious clues we had found near Liza's dad's shop, so that maybe—just *maybe*—we could crack this case before I lost two of my best friends.

But let me tell you, it wasn't easy. There didn't seem to be any obvious connection between the beads, the tracks, and the matchbox, and I had absolutely *nada* when it came to that strange glittery stuff we'd seen on the leaves.

What could have left that behind? What did it mean? Did it even mean anything?

No joke, I felt like I was on the verge of spraining a neuron. And worse, I felt dumb. Like I just wasn't clever enough, or logical enough, or *smart* enough. And that made me mad—it made me feel utterly, completely, totally *useless*!

I mean, let's face facts. There probably *was* some psycho arsonist running around Boca Falls, playing tag with matches. And if I wasn't so thickheaded, I might be able to figure out who the heck they were and help track them the heck down before Ernie and Liza were dragged off to different sides of the country. I almost banged my head against the passenger-side window, I was so annoyed at myself.

"Something frying your coco, Jorge?" asked my grandpa, bringing me out of my thoughts.

I shrugged, staring out at the blue-green blur of trees and sky. "Nah, it's nothing."

"Doesn't seem like nothing. Seems more like *some*thing. In fact, you think any harder and I'm afraid it's gonna leave a mark."

The brown, sun-toasted skin around my abuelo's eyes crinkled a little as he smiled at me, and for some reason that made me feel a little better. Or at least a little less hopeless.

"Grandpa, can I ask you something?"

"Sure."

"What do you think about that old town curse? That whole haunted piñata legend?"

"Well, I'm not gonna lie," he said, running a hand through his thick, white hair. "It's definitely a scary story. But the truth is that you and me live under the same roof as something much, *much* scarier . . . your grandma."

"Ha. Yeah." He made a good point. "I guess what I'm trying to ask is, do you think it could be true? Do you think it's possible a haunted piñata could actually exist?" Yep. That's where I was at the moment. Debating the possible existence of a supernatural, fire-spitting party decoration. Talk about desperate.

My grandpa was making his "thinking cap" face.

"You know, now that you mention it, way back when, there used to be this super smart girl here in town—Emilia Peterson, I think her name was—who claimed she'd seen the piñata monster. I think she was a friend of that Blackbriar boy. I always thought she seemed like a nice enough kid, but of course, I didn't believe her, and still don't. Now, I'm not gonna sit here and pretend to know everything that is or isn't out there. That'd be silly. But having said that, I'd be *extremely* surprised if there really is a haunted piñata lurking around town." He glanced sideways at me with one bushy black eyebrow raised in the shape of a caterpillar. "Hey, you're not worried about the farm, are you? Remember, we've lived here for over fifty years—cincuenta años—and we never had any problems. No fire, nothing. And if you're worried about yourself, the only kid I ever heard was eaten by that monster got swallowed headfirst, which, in your case, is gonna be pretty much impossible."

I sighed. Can you believe I had to put up with cabezón jokes from my own grandfather? ¡Órale!

"Maybe you should think about going into stand-up comedy," I told him as he playfully ruffled my hair, cracking up at his own cheesy joke.

"I hope that's not what's bothering you," he said.

"Nah, it's not that. It's not *exactly* that." I turned in the seat to face him, feeling kind of . . . I don't know—vulnerable? "Abuelo, have you ever felt like you're just not smart enough?"

"All the time," he said. "It's a big part of being a married man."

"Funny. But seriously, though. All my life people have been telling me that I'm not smart, that I'm stupid because I can't ace some math test or I don't know what element comes after boron on the periodic table. But I've always kind of known deep down inside that there're all kinds of smart, so I never believed them. That is, until now."

My abuelo gave me a sympathetic look. "Jorge, don't say that. You're a very intelligent boy. *Muy inteligente*. Besides, you should never hold someone else's opinion about yourself higher than your own, because no one knows you like *you*. And most of the time when someone makes you feel small, it's just their own sad way of trying to make themselves feel big. Nada más." He nudged me with his arm. "By the way, who told you that you were stupid?"

"Grandma did. Just now, before we left!"

My abuelo nodded like he'd suddenly remembered (and hadn't been standing two feet away when she'd said it). "Bueno, you *did* almost break her favorite mug."

"It was an accident! The Pop-Tart burned my fingers when I went to take it out, and I yanked my arm back!"

"Yo sé, yo sé . . . but you really shouldn't count your grandmother. She thinks *everybody's* tonto. Me included." He nudged me again. "Jorge, I'm gonna let you in on a little secret: 'Poco a poco, se anda lejos. Little by little, one goes far.' What I'm trying to say is that there's no such thing as smart people or stupid people. Just people who are committed to something and those who aren't. And if you stick with something long enough—whatever that thing may be—you'll come up with ideas and solutions that not even a so-called genius could've thought of."

CHAPTER 24

My grandpa's little pep talk had done a pretty good job of cheering me up. Still, I wasn't smiling much as I swept the floors inside what was left of Liza's dad's butcher shop.

The place was hardly more than a blackened skeleton now, the floor tiles scorched with smoke, the ceiling beams caved in and cracked like badly busted ribs.

It was really tough seeing it like this. I had some pretty cool memories in here. This was where I'd first come to score some grub for

Carter. This was the place Liza and I had first hit it off as buds. Heck, even my abuela liked to shop here, and she pretty much hated everything! Liza's family had built something special. A landmark. Kind of like the Hollywood Walk of Fame back in L.A., only "beefier." But now all that hard work—all those years of blood, sweat, and tears—was gone. *Poof!* Just like that. I could only imagine what she and her dad must've been going through.

As I swept an ashy path toward what used to be the prep area (where Liza had once caught me sneaking around), I could feel tears burning behind my eyes. I tried to tell myself that it was just all the gritty stuff swirling in the air, but it's kind of hard to lie to yourself.

"Jorge, watch out for nails," my grandpa called from the other side of the shop. "There's clavos all over the place. And your grandma's going to kill you if I have to pay the hospital twenty bucks to give you a tetanus shot."

Yep. That sounded like my sweet ole nana.

"I'll be careful," I started to say, and then *clunk!* The head of my broomstick crashed into something.

Something hard.

Something heavy.

It was buried deep beneath a pile of blackened rubble, maybe two feet from where the back door had stood, and it really didn't want to budge.

So naturally, I decided to investigate . . .

And what did I find? The lock/handle combo for the back door. The door the authorities believed the arsonist had broken in through.

But it wasn't the fact I'd found it, or even its surprising unmelted-ness that had me staring, that had my heart doing Simone Biles–level cartwheels in my chest.

It was what I'd noticed about it. Just a tiny little detail, really—but a detail that would change *everything*.

The lockset was *un*locked!

CHAPTER 25

Liza and I turned to him. "You did?" I asked, surprised.

"Yeah. I kind of just suspect everyone now," Ernie admitted.

"Even me?" Carter looked confused.

Ernie gave an embarrassed nod. "You do act pretty sus at times."

"Guys, focus!" I shouted, practically slamming the lockset into Liza's hands. "Check this out! See? It's unlocked!"

Liza shrugged. "So?"

"*So?* It's our smoking gun! That's the lockset from the back door of your dad's shop!"

Now Ernie shrugged. "So?"

"*So?* Don't either of you two get it? One of the big reasons why most people in this kooky town are *sooo* convinced the fire is the work of the haunted piñata is because Cathy the shop manager *distinctly* remembers having locked the back door! Which, if she did, means nobody but some kind of supernatural monstruo could have gotten in! But that thing in your hand proves someone *could have!*"

The brilliant little hamster inside of Liza's head finally hopped on its hamster wheel and got going.

Her eyes narrowed sharply on mine. "And you found it just like this?" she asked me.

"Just like that! It was buried underneath part of a collapsed wall."

"No one could've messed with it, then?"

"Nope! And Cathy said it herself: only she and your dad had a key. And it's supposedly a brand-new state-of-the-art lockset, right? Well, if that's the case, there's probably only a *tiny* handful of people who could've picked it, and even fewer whose creepy, toothy grin has 'evil local arsonist' written all over it."

"You're talking about Linus Lester," said Liza. "Linus the locksmith. The guy at the bodega."

"That's *exactly* who I'm talking about!"

"Jorge's pretty inteligente, huh?" Carter said with a toothy smile. I'd already laid out my theory to the big guy and he'd given it his fangy seal of approval.

I dapped up my chupacabra buddy. "Gracias. Oh, and don't forget all those weirdo looks he was giving us back at the bodega. The guy was practically hanging on every word we said! And you want to know why? Because the villain was worried we might be onto him!"

"But wasn't he with Ms. B. at the time of the fire?"

said Ernie. "Helping her with her alarm system or whatever?"

Liza jiggled the handle unit, thinking. Then she said, "Unless he *wasn't*."

"You think dey both lying to our faces?" Carter whispered, looking suddenly furious. Claws out. Fangs bared.

Note to self: *never* lie to a chupacabra. Apparently they no likey.

"Not necessarily," said Liza. "Linus and Ms. Blanco only live a few miles from the shop. It's not impossible that right after helping her, he could've jumped into his car, sped over, broken in, and started the fire."

"Heck, he could've even set off her alarm system on purpose," I pointed out. "To make her come over so he'd have an airtight alibi. And *then* he could've sped over to the shop!" It would've been a tight squeeze timewise, sure. But not outside the realm of possibility.

"Hey, you might be onto something, Jorge," Ernie said, nodding along now. "I'm not gonna lie—my money is still on the haunted piñata, but if it's not the undead, candy-stuffed reincarnation of Miguel

Valdez Blackbriar, then it's *definitely* this guy! He ticks all the bad guy boxes!"

Liza, meanwhile, was grinning at me like a sugar addict who'd just been handed the keys to Willy Wonka's famous factory. "Jorge, I think you've just Sherlocked our villain. Now we just have to prove it!"

Bad Guy Boxes

☑ Creepy vibes
☑ Sneaky eyes
☑ Villainous XXL teeth

CHAPTER 26

Our entire case boiled down to a single thing: evidence. We needed concrete, undeniable, *irrefutable* evidence of Linus Lester's fire-starting ways. I'm talking the kind of fingerprints-on-doorknobs stuff that could prove the locksmith creep was behind the fires and get him thrown behind bars.

The only catch? Getting our hands on that kind of evidence wasn't going to be easy. As a matter of fact, the only way seemed to be by busting into the creep's place of business—his large private warehouse way over on the east end of Boca Falls. But, as they say, it was time to fight fire with fire. Figuratively speaking, of course.

Before we could unleash our inner Tom Cruises, though, and go all *Mission: Impossible* on that joint, we needed to make sure that in the unhappy event we were spotted by some hidden security cameras or something, our identities would be kept secret from the world.

Translation: it was superhero dress-up time!

We had three disguises to choose from, and we laid them all out on Ernie's bed later that night.

Two were Ernie's old Halloween costumes: a Batman mask plus cape and grapple gun; and a Spider-Man mask with matching stretchy shirt. The other was Liza's Electra costume, complete with red forearm wraps and a cool bandana face covering.

"Dude, I can't be Batman without the utility belt," I told Ernie. "That's like Ben without Jerry. I'll flip you for Spider-Man."

"No deal," he said.

Next to me, frowning a little, Carter asked, "Where's my superhero costume?"

And Liza said, "You were born with it, bud."

Anyway, it was funny how the simple act of putting on an awesomely cool superhero costume could make you feel like you've jumped straight into the pages of a comic book . . .

Fifteen minutes later

Things to avoid

THERE'S NO WAY IN, JORGE! YOU'RE NOT REALLY BATMAN AND THIS THING DOESN'T REALLY WORK.

CORRECTION: THERE'S NO WAY THAT YOU, ME, OR LIZA CAN CLIMB THAT FENCE!

IT'S SUPACARTER TIME!

HEY, AT LEAST ONE OF US IS A REAL SUPERHERO.

Liza leaned cautiously over a small glass bowl sitting on a mini stove. A mysterious-looking dark powder glittered inside. "Looks like some kind of metal salt," she said curiously.

I frowned. "Metal salt?" I'd never heard of that. But it certainly didn't sound like something you wanted to go sprinkling on your french fries, that's for sure.

Suddenly, a flash of realization lit up Liza's eyes and she shook her head disbelievingly as she said, "Oh my gosh . . ."

"¿Qué? What's up?"

"It's a pyrotechnic colorant!" she explained (like that meant anything to me). "A color enhancer for flames. I used something like it a couple of years ago in my second-place science fair project."

"Hold up. *You* got second place in a science fair?" I said, honestly shocked.

"Total rip-off, right? But those things can be super political." Then, turning back to the bowl, she began cranking up the temperature on the mini stove. "Observe . . ." she whispered, sounding exactly like every mad scientist in every movie *ever*. An instant later—*WHOOSH!*—the metallic salt suddenly burst up in a shimmering cloud, all big and green and sparkly!

"*Green flames!*" Ernie cried, squeezing in between us. "It's . . . it's HAUNTED PIÑATA MAGIC!" The amount of fearful tremble in his voice would've made a harp string jealous.

Liza, on the other hand, was all smiles. Or at least her eyes were smiling. "A little flame colorant to give an old creepy legend some serious oomph!"

"Enough oomph to terrorize an entire town," I said as it dawned on me.

Meanwhile, a few feet away, Carter was busy climbing all over some giant shrink-wrapped box?

Container?

Something.

Then he began sniffing at it and clawing wildly at its corners.

"Carter, get over here!" I whisper-shouted. "Check this out!"

But the overgrown mosquito ignored me.

He was way too into whatever was inside that box.

"Dis smells funny," he growled, really going after the plastic wrap now, like a dog digging an escape tunnel under a fence.

"Bro, stop messing around!" I hissed at him. "You're making me nervous!"

A split second later, the snooping chupacabra went tumbling backward off the thing, taking most of the plastic wrap with him and revealing a big square-shaped trash bin as he crash-landed (huge emphasis on *CRRRASH!*) into a pile of metal buckets a few feet away.

A huge freestanding shelf he'd smacked into began to wobble dangerously, and for one terrible moment, I thought it was going over.

Was absolutely positive, in fact!

But someway, somehow, it settled.

"*Phew*, that was close!" Ernie said, sighing in relief.

You can say that again, Spidey.

Next thing I knew, Carter was on his feet again, diving headfirst into the trash bin. He came out holding what looked like a whole bushel of not-so-lively-looking lab mice by the ends of their long, skinny tails.

"See?" Carter said, grinning like a fox in a hen-house. "Smells funny."

"Hey, those look just like the mice you found in

the woods!" Ernie exclaimed, and he wasn't lying. All half dozen or so ratones were as stiff as statues—just like the ones near Liza's dad's shop! It was another unmistakable clue.

We all quickly hurried over, gathering around him.

"It looks like someone hit them with Mr. Freeze's ice ray!" I rasped.

"Easy there, Bruce Wayne. Ice rays don't exist in this metaverse." Liza took one of the mice by its tail—total grossfest, I know—and began inspecting it with squinted eyes. "But something's definitely up with these critters."

All of a sudden, from somewhere behind us, I heard Carter shout, "Check this out! Found some live ones, too!"

Man, this dude was all over the place!

Now he was a few feet away, crouching beside a large steel cage filled with little white mice.

Next, his long bony fingers pried open the cage, and a split second later a stampede of tiny pink feet came rushing out in an excited chorus of chitters. The mice scattered to all corners of the warehouse.

"That's it. It's gotta be him!" Ernie whisper-shouted,

whipping around to face me. His eyes were glittering with triumph. "I mean, the green flames. The petrified mice. The locksmith *has* to be the arborist! How much more evidence do we need?"

"You mean *arsonist*," corrected Liza. "An arborist trims trees. But yeah, it's got to be him!"

I was right there with them.

We had our man!

"As the saying goes," I said. "'Where there's smoke, there's fire!'"

Carter, meanwhile, had moved on to another workbench, messing with what looked like an industrial-size Bunsen burner now.

I had just opened my mouth to shout, "Dude, settle down before I put you back on your leash!" when a foot-long tongue of flame, green and sizzling, burst up right in the chupacabra's face, and he leapt back with a panicked screech.

The big guy's big back slammed hard into a nearby shelf, and just like last time, the shelf began to wobble . . .

And wobble . . .

But unlike last time—well, I'll just let you guess what happened . . .

CHAPTER 27

Twenty minutes later, Batman, Spider-Man, Electra, and a bloodsucking Chewbacca arrived at Commissioner Gordon's office—er, at the Boca Falls firehouse—via the Batmobile. (All right, *fine* . . . via a plain old city bus.)

The fire chief was sitting at his desk inside a small office next to the garage.

He looked curiously up at us (and *especially* at Carter) when we rushed in.

"I don't mean to be rude or anything," he said, "but, geez Louise, that's one strange-lookin' pooch!"

"Forget my dog!" I said. "We know who the arsonist is!"

Kenneth blinked like we'd just asked him to hand over the keys to his fire engine so we could take it for a joyride. "Excuse me? *What* arsonist?"

Was he kidding?

I glared at him like, *C'mon, dude!* "The one who's been setting fires all over Boca Falls! Who else?"

"Who told you an arsonist was responsible for the fires?"

This, no surprise, made Ernie go all Mount Vesuvius. With his Spider-Man mask pushed halfway up his face, he erupted, "Oh, snap out of it, man! There's no such thing as a haunted piñata! How else could the fires have been started? It's the work of an arsonist! AN ARSONIST, I tell ya!"

"Fire chief, please tell me you don't actually believe in that ridiculous town legend," Liza practically pleaded with him.

Chief Kenneth crossed his muscular arms over his muscular chest in a *try me* pose. "Until I'm presented with evidence to the contrary, that ridiculous town superstition is the only thing I have to go on."

"You want evidence?" At my signal, Ernie quickly dug the case-breaking lockset out of his backpack, handing it to me, and I, in turn, handed it to the fire chief. "There's your evidence."

Boom. Mic drop.

"And here's some more!" said Ernie, digging a

handful of the metallic salt out of his pocket and sprinkling it, chef-style, onto the chief's desk.

"And there's your third piece of evidence," I said as the terrified mouse scampered, chittering, down the side of the desk and into a hole in the wall. "Well, there it goes . . ."

"*Whoa, whoa, whoa!*" shouted the chief, throwing his hands up with a huff. "Is this some kind of joke?"

"It's no joke!" I told him. "I found that lockset inside her dad's butcher shop—*open* just like that! And who else in town has the skills to pick it?"

Pointing at the mound o' pyrotechnic salt, Liza said, "We found that inside Linus's own warehouse! It's a colorant, which just so happens to turn fire the *exact* shade of green as all those supposed haunted piñata fires!"

"And don't forget the mice!" Ernie jumped in. "We found a couple of petrified ones in the woods near the crime scene and a mother lode in a trash can in that creep's place!"

The look of shock that had come over the chief's face was so over-the-top and so cartoonish that you would've thought he'd just jammed a finger into an electrical outlet. He glared at us in disbelief. "Hold on. You three *broke into* Linus's warehouse?!"

"What else were we supposed to do?!" I snapped. "Send an email asking him to ship us proof of his guiltiness?"

Kenneth sat back, scolding us through the slits of his eyes. "East Boca Falls can be a dangerous place at night. There are coyotes out there and it's all big warehouses with no one around. You were playing with fire."

"Actually, it's the *playing with fire* part we were

investigating," I grumbled, but the fire chief just ignored me.

He said, "Not to mention the fact that Linus has dogs. *Mean* ones. You could've gotten yourselves hurt."

"We know about the dogs," Liza told him. "They're actually cool people."

"Oh, so you know about the dogs, huh? Well, do you also know that breaking and entering is a serious crime punishable by *jail time*?"

"*Technically* we didn't break anything," said Ernie. "Well, except for a few of his shelves and stuff, but that was totally an accident."

The chief looked tired. He let out a tired sigh. Then his tired eyes dropped to his watch and he looked even more tired. "Look, while I appreciate your . . . enthusiasm, I have enough to worry about without costumed kiddie vigilantes sneaking into warehouses and destroying private property. Now, if I can please just get three promises that all of you will go straight home and do your best to follow all of our town's longstanding civil ordinances in the future, I'll do my best to make sure you stay out of trouble."

"But what about Linus Lester?" Liza asked.

"What about him?"

"Aren't you going to *do* anything?"

"I would," he said, "if I actually thought he was guilty."

If? IF? What more do ya need? A signed CONFESSION?!

The fire chief shut his eyes, pinching the bridge of his nose. "Do any of you know what happens to metal under extreme temperatures?" he asked us after a long moment.

"Uh, it melts?" I guessed.

"That is correct. Under extreme heat, metal melts. In other words, metals—like most substances—

expand or contract with changes in temperature. Now, you may be asking yourselves, why on earth is he giving us a lesson in thermal expansion? The answer is simple: if any of you had spent *any* time as a firefighter, you'd know that the rapid heating and cooling of locksets can cause them to randomly lock or unlock. Which is why they are not admissible as evidence in any court of law. The fact that you found this particular lockset unlocked"—he held it up— "proves absolutely *nothing*, except for the simple fact that it was, at some point, subjected to extreme heat."

Huh. Did not know that. There was a short silence while the four of us absorbed the surprise science lesson. Then Liza said, "But what about the pyrotechnic compound? It's the *same* color as all the fires! Don't you think that's more than a little coincidental?"

"Coincidental, yes. Damning, no. Poison green, which I'm assuming is the color produced by the metallic salts you've illegally procured and so generously scattered all over my desk, is probably the second or third most popular firework colorant in the world. And you three might not be aware of this, but Linus is in charge of running all our town's firework displays. I know, because I recommended him myself to the city council."

Huh. Did not know that, either.

"But what about the mice?" Ernie cried. "Only a villain would breed that many mice!"

"While I'm not a fan of rodents myself," said the chief, "did any of you stop to consider Linus's line of work? He creates security devices of all kinds, and he specializes in both locks and motion-sensor technology. And what better way to test your latest security gizmo than against the sneakiest thieves on Earth?"

Hmm. That was a good point. In fact, *all* his points were good. Unfortunately.

"What's more, I can personally assure you that Linus had nothing to do with what happened to the butcher shop."

"Why do you say that?" Liza asked.

"Because he was with me on the morning of the fire."

"He was?"

"He called me to take a look at a circuit breaker box near his home. Some of the wiring had shorted and it posed a fire hazard. I'm telling you—you three are barking up the wrong tree." His gaze narrowed uncertainly on Carter again, who had just finished obeying his thirst and was strolling awkwardly over on all fours, his fancy tag jingling. "Hey, you sure that's a dog?"

"He's mixed," I said.

"With *what*? A Komodo dragon?"

More silence. Longer this time. Probably noticing how disappointed we all looked, the chief leaned toward us and said, in a soft, encouraging voice, "Look, you three did good work. I'm not saying you didn't. Your spunk and go-getter spirits are more than commendable. I wish I had a dozen more like you here in the firehouse." His tired blue eyes flicked to Liza. "And I'm truly sorry about what happened to your dad's shop. I really am. But that's why detective work should be left up to detectives. It's better for everyone that way."

Guess it was, I thought.

A moment later, as we filed dejectedly out of his office, I heard the fire chief say (and sounding pretty sorry for us, too), "Cool costumes, by the way!"

As you can probably imagine, all four of us were

feeling pretty bummed out and defeated as we started back home.

Sadly, our big lead had turned out to be a big, fat nada-burger. The mice, the metal salts, the unlocked deadbolt I'd found—*nada*. All of it easily explained away. Super easily, as a matter of fact. But honestly, what did we expect? This was a super spooky, super TWISTY town legend that had gone unsolved for forty years! Did we seriously believe three kids and their chupacabra buddy would be able to crack it in less than *five* days?

Yeah. Not likely.

Heck, in a way, it was almost kind of funny. Just thirty minutes ago, the locksmith dude's warehouse had seemed like the evil laboratory of some criminal mastermind, and the locksmith dude himself couldn't have looked any guiltier if he'd been wearing the Hamburglar's striped pj's and mask. On the bright side, at least we could cross another name off our list of suspects.

Baron von Belcherstaub

Ms. Blanco

The locksmith creep

So that was exactly three down, and only about 59,997 possible suspects to go. Easy-peasy.

The night was warm and my Batman cape was already beginning to chafe my neck as we made our way up Montaña Street, kicking rocks and not really talking much.

We were maybe twelve blocks from Ernie's house when I stooped to pick up a fat brown pine cone, getting ready to chuck it fastball-style into the trees to our left—

And saw something.

Only at first, I wasn't even sure *what* I saw.

At first, I thought it might be some big ole buck hanging out near the edge of the woods, munching on grass or whatever it is that big ole bucks munch on. But it was no buck.

I stopped dead in my tracks.

I blinked.

I rubbed my eyes.

I stared.

I did a double take—no, a *triple* take! Because there, looming in the trees not fifty yards away, all big and hulking and absolutely *terrifying*, was a monster!

And more specifically, a *HAUNTED PIÑATA MON-STER!*

CHAPTER 28

Or at least it *looked* like a haunted piñata monster! The creature—or donkey, or thing, or whatever!—was as huge as a house, with squat, tree-trunk-thick legs and eyes that burned so fiery in the gloomy darkness of the woods that they probably would've given Smokey Bear a heart attack.

The monster's "fur," what looked like a skin-crawling combination of papier-mâché and matted hair, rippled in the breeze, and its many colors—red and yellow and pink and blue—were not the usual cheerful shades. No, these were the deepest, darkest, most *spine-tingling* colors I had ever seen!

By the way, if you never thought a color could turn your knees to jelly and make your insides shrivel up like deep-fried chicharrones—well, welcome to the club. I never thought so, either.

As I watched, totally petrified and hardly able to breathe, the thing began moving, slipping silently and creepily through the rows of dark trees.

Then, suddenly, it slid into a patch of inky shadows and vanished into thin air!

"Jorge, what's wrong?" I heard a voice say, sounding very far away.

Liza.

It was Liza's voice.

A moment later, her worried-looking face filled my vision and she said, "Hey, are you okay? You look like you've seen a ghost."

I realized I wasn't breathing. I'd been holding my breath for who knows how long. Letting it out slowly through my mouth, I said, "Try a haunted piñata."

Ernie and Carter had both stopped walking and were staring back at me. Now their lips began to curl up into small smiles like they were waiting for some hilarious punchline. But when the punchline didn't come, the smiles quickly turned upside down.

"Jorge, you trying to make a funny?" asked Ernie, sounding (and looking) a wee bit concerned.

"Didn't any of you see it?" I pointed a shaky finger toward the woods—toward where I'd seen the thing.

"It was right in those trees. Just over there."

Please say yes...

But they all shook their heads.

Ugh.

"Jorge, you *sure* you saw it?" whispered Carter. His mismatched eyes were jacked wide with worry.

"I . . ." Was I? Now I wasn't sure. I mean, I *thought* I'd seen it. But then again . . . where had it gone? And why hadn't anyone else seen it?

I could feel panic rising in my throat like a bad gas station burrito, but I forced it back down.

C'mon, dude, get a grip! I said to myself. *This is ridículo! Just plain old silly!*

The fact was, those woods were loaded with wild animals. Hundreds of them. *Thousands!* Why couldn't it have been Bambi's weird-looking cousin that I'd seen? Why did my imagination always have to take everything to the wildest, scariest, most ridiculous extreme?

"Jorge?"

Pushing my Batman mask halfway up my face, I blinked dazedly at Liza. "Yeah?"

"Well, did you?"

"I . . . I don't know. Probably not. Probably just my

imagination running wild on me." I tried to force a shaky smile to my face. But I'm not so sure it got there.

"Maybe it was a deer?" she said.

"Yeah, maybe. I mean, probably."

"I can smell some deer close by," Carter said helpfully.

"And I once saw a deer not too far from here," added Ernie—a little *less* helpfully.

Liza patted me on the arm, giving me the ole "I feel for ya, kid" type of look. "Hey, we've all been under a lot of stress lately. And the mind can play some pretty mean tricks on you when you're super stressed. It's natural. Happens to everyone . . . *Bruce*."

"Ha. I—yeah, you're right," I said, slipping my Batman mask back on and feeling a bit better. "C'mon . . . let's get out of here before I start seeing the Joker and Bane running around out here."

CHAPTER 29

Over the next couple of weeks things went from bad to worse. We didn't turn up a single new lead, and every other day there was talk of another fuego—a burning field or someone's barn that had mysteriously caught fire. The newspapers were boiling over with it:

THE HAUNTED PIÑATA STRIKES AGAIN!

THE DEMON IS ON A WARPATH!

VENGEFUL MIGUEL VALDEZ BLACKBRIAR
IS ANGRIER THAN EVER!
IS BOCA FALLS PAYING
FOR ITS PAST SINS?

The *Boca Tribune*, Raymond Rathbone's news-paper, was especially on top of everything. Its motto was "Mañana's News, Today," and they pretty much lived up to the hype, always breaking the latest stories.

The *Tribune* published two papers and two special editions each day, which were delivered by Mr. Rathbone's fleet of high-tech delivery drones. And they always had a bunch of reporters running tirelessly around Boca, digging for the latest scoop.

Under the constant barrage of scary headlines and scarier happenings, the whole town was more jittery than a cockroach at an exterminator's convention.

And when people get that jittery, they run for protection.

Or at least for what they *think* will protect them.

So it was no big surprise that Ms. Blanco's anti-piñata beads became the hottest fashion accessory in town, and that two-hour-plus lines outside of Linus Lester's shop were the norm—folks snapping up locks, motion sensors, and video doorbells like they were going out of style.

School wasn't much of a distraction, either. No one wanted to talk about anything except the old Blackbriar curse, and the teachers and hall monitors seemed to think everything in town was suddenly combustible.

To add fuel to the fire (pardon the pun), it wasn't long before haunted piñata sightings became as common as belt buckles in Boca. You really couldn't go anywhere without running into somebody who claimed to have seen the monster.

And it wasn't long before everyone in town started looking like a suspect. Grandmas included.

On the bright side—if there even *was* a bright side—at least I wasn't the only person around here who thought they'd seen el monstruo. Though the sheer number of sightings was kind of sort of making me wonder if maybe I did see it.

Pretty soon the whole town was choking on smoke and fear. Everybody was on edge, waiting for the next shoe to drop. Or, more specifically, for the next field or building to go up in flames. And those were the brave ones. The rest had already packed up their SUVs and said, "¡Adiós, Boca Falls!"

FOR SALE signs were popping up like weeds. They were everywhere. In front of at least a couple houses on every block, in half of the store windows. But it wasn't until one sprouted up in Liza's front yard that things got real.

"Want me to take it out to da woods and hide it where nobody find it?" Carter asked Liza, as the three of us stared miserably at the stupid sign.

"Unfortunately, that won't fix things," Liza said, looking totally depressed. "My dad will just put up another one."

You could tell Liza's whole world was crumbling around her. It was easy to see. At least it was easy for *me* to see, because I had so much experience with that feeling.

C'mon, honey. Time to go. You know the drill by now.

I knew exactly what it felt like to be uprooted from the place you called home. To be ripped right out of the ground like an unwanted tree and dragged away from everything familiar. But the worst part? There was nothing I could do to keep one of my best friends from experiencing that same awful feeling.

"What if this is it for our gang?" Ernie asked, staring dejectedly down at his sneakers. "What if it's all *hasta luego*s from here?"

Ignoring the growing galactic-size black hole in my gut, I put my arm around him and tried to be the rock our crew needed right now. "That's not going to happen," I said. "Nobody's going anywhere."

Only deep down inside, I knew the truth. And the truth was this: If we didn't figure out who—or maybe even *what*—was behind the fires, *and* put a stop to them, Liza, Ernie, Carter, and I would probably never see each other again. We certainly wouldn't be able to hang out on the regular anymore.

And the cherry on top of this sundae of awfulness? I was already beginning to blame myself for it. For everything. Just like I always did.

You're a jinx, said some annoying little voice inside my head. *You're the reason your mom has had such a tough life, why your dad left. Why this whole town is going up in flames.*

It didn't matter that I knew none of that stuff was actually true. Those accusing thoughts still came, and they still stung just as bad.

Even my abuela noticed my plummeting mood later that night at dinner.

"Hey, why you cryin'?" she asked me, her eyebrows screwed up like an annoyed question mark.

"I'm not *crying*," I groaned. "I'm worried."

"Worried about what?" asked Grandpa Patricio, putting down his fork.

"Worried the fires won't stop. Worried I'm going to lose my friends." Again. As usual.

Man, why didn't humans come up with something like those surge protector thingies for your emotions? I thought. That way we wouldn't have to feel so messed up inside all the time.

"What you need is a good old-fashioned pep talk," my abuela said, gesturing at me with her cup of atole. But when I stared at her, expecting to hear some pearls of old-school wisdom, she just shrugged and said, "Hey, don't look at me. I ain't good at that kinda stuff!"

I sighed. "Thanks a bunch, Grans."

"Look, Jorge, we're Mexican, okay? We're *Latinos*. We don't do that whole cup-is-half-full nonsense. We tell it like it is. So here's what my mother used to tell me: 'Stir the mole or get your butt out of the kitchen!'"

"What's that supposed to mean?"

"It means, you either fix what's bothering you, or you forget it!" She cut herself a neat little slice of flan (my grandma's specialty) and paused with a forkful halfway to her mouth. "Besides, look at it this way: if your friends leave, you'll have more time to spend with us."

I dropped my frowning face into my hands. "That's what I'm worried about!"

CHAPTER 30

As much as it pained me to admit it, my grandma was right. I needed to bust out of my funk, stop wasting time and energy stressing, and just put all my effort into actual productive stuff. Fight fire with fire, basically.

So that's exactly what I did. After a quick huddle with my bloodsucking best bud, the two of us decided to spend every waking moment—up to the very *second* when Liza's dad stuck her on a plane with a departure ticket in her hand—trying to crack this case. And that was on top of the time we were already spending trying to crack it with Liza and Ernie.

Anyway, that night while sleuthing on the interwebs, we came across this creepy fan site on all things Blackbriar. Among its two hundred or so disturbing yet info-packed pages, we saw scans of old newspaper articles about the fire and a bunch of interviews of the supposed eyewitnesses.

There was Luna Thorne, who had been the Blackbriars' maid for almost ten years, and Reginald Stevens, their butler, who had been with them even longer. There was also the Blackbriars' personal bodyguard, a Mr. Jaxon Randall, and Miguel's uncle, Benjamin Blackbriar. Oh, and Miguel's cousin, Elijah Blackbriar, who also claimed to have seen the haunted piñata.

The most interesting part, I guess, was how closely their descriptions of the piñata all matched, and also how closely they matched the description Ms. Blanco gave us. But other than that, nothing we came across flipped any *Aha!* switches in my brain. Too bad there wasn't a page called *Identity of the arsonist revealed!* because that would've made things a whole lot easier.

At any rate, we decided to go over all the clues again and try to find the common denominator. If there even was one. Our list looked something like this:

#1—the dozen or so anti-piñata charm beads

#2—the strange glittery stuff on the leaves

#3—the even stranger Rollerblade-like tracks

#4—the pack of matches from the baron's bank

#5—the pair of "petrified" mice Carter had been
so obsessed with

#6—the ink-stained hanky he'd found in the bushes

Okay, so those last two didn't really strike me as clues, but Carter was convinced they were, and I didn't want to burst the big guy's bubble.

Our main problem, though? We couldn't make heads or tails of them! They really didn't seem connected *at all.* And most of the time I just found myself getting more and more frustrated.

There were other questions, too, of course. Important ones. Like, who had Red seen walking in the woods that night? And who—or *what*—had Cathy, the manager of the butcher shop, spotted lurking in the trees? And what had Ms. Blanco encountered all those years ago in the woods? And why was I so hungry?

Okay. That last one wasn't relevant to the case. But note to self: pick up a couple of Snickers bars from the grocery.

Moving on . . .

What was up with the six-year haunting cycles?

Why six years? And, probably most important of all, how did they get away with it for forty years? Why hadn't they ever been caught?

Ugh.

Talk about a total brain buster. Those detective shows made it seem so easy, too.

In fact, I was getting so frustrated with everything that I did the unthinkable: I decided to go to Paz for help.

She was sitting out on the porch, reading a magazine in her rocking chair, when I found her.

"Grandma, what do you know about the Blackbriar case?"

Paz's eyes screwed up at me, real suspicious-like. "Who's asking?"

I made a big show of looking around. "Me! Who else?"

She took a dip into her think tank for a sec, then a sly, sneaky look I didn't really trust crept slowly over her face. "How 'bout this?" she said in her most sincere voice. "I'll tell you *all* the juicy details if you wash and detail my car."

Ha! I might've been born at night, but it wasn't *last* night! "Ah, forget it!" I snapped.

Anyway, suffice to say Carter and I really weren't getting anywhere. We were about as close to solving this case as we were to Pluto. (Which, by the way, is approximately 3.28 billion miles from Earth.)

Fortunately, though, there was someone on our team who was a *teensy bit* closer . . .

CHAPTER 31

The following afternoon, I got a call from Liza. She wanted us all over at her house, and *pronto*!

It was like walking onto a set of *CSI: Miami.* *Seriously.* I almost didn't even believe my—

Wait.

Hold up.

"Yo, why is my picture up here under 'Suspects'?!" I snapped at Liza.

"Because I made *everyone* a suspect, Jorge. It's how all the pros do it. But don't worry, I cleared you pretty early on."

Pretty early on?! "You should've cleared me *first!*"

"Actually, I cleared Carter first," she said. "I mean, how can you not trust that face?"

Beside me, Carter was now grinning and nodding like he totally agreed.

"She has a point, you know," Ernie told me.

Bah. Whatever.

I continued perusing Liza's recently decorated "wall o' suspects."

"Hey, these are all the people who claimed to have seen the haunted piñata," I said to Liza.

"That's them. The ones closest to the Blackbriars, anyway."

Spotting Zane's picture up by her closet door, I

PERSONS OF INTEREST

Reginald Stevens

Blackbriars' butler

Benjamin Blackbriar

Miguel's uncle

Emilia Peterson

Miguel's childhood friend

Elijah Blackbriar

Miguel's cousin

Luna Thorne

Blackbriars' maid

Jaxon Randall

Blackbriars' personal bodyguard

said, "I still think *that's* the twerp behind it."

"How come you have old Mr. Splinter up here under 'Possibles'?" asked Ernie, pointing at a different (and *much* larger) group of pictures on the ceiling above Liza's bed.

"That's my list of secondary suspects," she said.

"But Mr. Splinter *died*. Last month."

"He did?"

"Uh, *yeah!* My parents even spoke at his funeral."

Liza frowned. "Darn it. He was my dark horse."

"I guess you can cross him off your list now," I told her. "But I hope that poor dead guy wasn't the reason you called us over."

"He wasn't," replied Boca's newest gumshoe. "*This* was." And turning on her heel she pointed excitedly up at another photograph up on the wall.

"That's Red Wilson," said Ernie.

Liza grinned. "Also known as our arsonist!"

"Wait, wait, hold up," I said. "You think *Red* is the arsonist? Based on what, exactly?"

"Well, it's not a slam dunk or anything, Jorge. It's just my hunch. My *strong* hunch. And it's a hunch based off the fact that he's a loner who has spent the last decade living out in the woods, all alone, *and* he has a pretty big bone to pick with Boca Falls . . ."

"Did someone say bone?" asked Carter, looking very hungry all of a sudden.

I shook my head. "Liza, what are you talking about?"

"Red was telling the truth," she explained. "He used to be a firefighter here in town. That is, until he did such a terrible job on the haunted piñata case— and on *purpose*, I strongly suspect—that they fired him. Then next thing you know, the bank calls in a few of his loans and he loses a fairly lucrative fireworks business."

Interesting. "A fireworks business, huh?"

"Uh-huh. In other words, easy access to the *exact* kind of stuff that would give the so-called 'haunted piñata' fires their spooky greenish color."

She was talking about the pyrotechnic colorants.

Hmm. Double interesting.

"And was it Baron von Belcherstaub's bank that called in the loans?" I asked, feeling like the puzzle pieces were beginning to fall into place.

"Exactly. You starting to see the picture here?"

Yeah. In stunning 8K, as a matter of fact.

"Plus, he tried to frame Ms. B., remember?" Liza

went on. "Claiming he'd seen her out there in the woods. And isn't that what guilty people *always* do? He was blowing smoke!"

"You mean literally?" asked Carter, confused.

"Well, no . . . not literally."

"I mean, he *did* try to blow us up," Ernie pointed out. "That's a pretty villain-y thing to do, isn't it?"

It was. The guy most definitely had a short fuse, pardon the pun.

"All right, look," I said. "I definitely smell what you're cookin' here, but none of this really *proves* anything. And please don't say you want to go busting into Red's double-wide in the woods, because that just ain't gonna happen!"

"No, I have a better idea," Liza said. "We're going to catch Red *red-handed*!"

CHAPTER 32

"Take a look at this." Liza's finger was aiming up at a large map of Boca Falls that had been stapled and thumbtacked onto the big corkboard next to her poster of Albert Einstein with his tongue sticking out. The twelve-by-fifteen rectangle of silk-coated paper was crisscrossed with string, dotted with colorful tacks and itty-bitty little flame stickers, which—I assumed—were supposed to represent the places and businesses that had been burned down or caught fire.

"I think I've cracked their pattern!" Liza announced with a magician-esque sweep of her arm.

Carter blinked like he'd just been given the longest word in a spelling bee. "*Whose* pattern? The arsonist's?"

"Uh-huh! Red's! Whoever!" Liza grabbed an

extra-long ruler and whipped it like a lightsaber toward the map, pointing stuff out as she spoke. "Pay special attention to the dates and locations! I labeled them for ease of reading."

"They're all over the place," Ernie said, squinting, trying to spot the hidden pattern.

"On the surface, sure. But look closer. Notice the dates of each of the attacks. Notice how a fire occurs at one end of town and then the next time at the opposite end."

It was kind of like staring at one of those Magic Eye illustrations. After a few seconds, *bam!* You saw it. "Okay, yeah... I get you," I said.

"It seems to me like our arsonist's strategy is to pick targets as far away from each other as possible," Liza explained. "Which makes sense because security is going to be tighter in an area right after an attack. Also, spreading the attacks all over Boca and working slowly toward the center of town is likely to make people feel surrounded, like the fires are closing in on them, which, in turn, is likely to fuel a town-wide panic and give this villain—erm, *Red*—his twisted kicks."

I'm not going to lie. Her theory made sense. In

fact, it made so much sense that it was starting to make dollars.

Carter's long, scaly tail wagged excitedly and his mismatched eyes looked on the verge of crossing as he stared up at the map like it was the final question on *Jeopardy!* "Hey, you smart as a raccoon!" he told Liza.

Liza smiled. "I'll take that! Anyway, if my theory is correct—and I see no reason to believe it isn't—their next strike should be right *here.*"

"This cluster of shops up near Verde Avenue. It's the furthest cluster of businesses from the last fire, which falls in line with the pattern, *and* it's a commercial area, whereas their last attack was residential, which also goes with the pattern."

She wasn't just making it up, either. It was all right there on her map, color coded and everything.

At any rate, Liza had convinced me. Now there's was only one question left. "So what do we do now? Call the police? Tell the fire chief?"

Liza gave her head a firm shake, the lenses of her glasses glinting as she said, "No. No one's going to listen to us. If we really want to stop this criminal—whoever it is—we'll have to do it *ourselves*."

"Wait, if you don't want to tell the police or the fire chief, then how exactly are you planning on stopping this maniac?"

"Yeah, what are you suggesting?" Ernie wanted to know.

A sneaky-sly smile had begun to spread slowly across Liza's face. A smile which told me that things were about to get *real*. "I'm suggesting we fight fire with fire."

"We can't do dat!" cried Carter in outrage. "Two wrongs don't make a right. Even chupacabras know dat!"

Liza smacked him with the whites of her eyes. "I didn't mean it like that."

"Then how'd you mean it?" I asked.

Liza's grin had widened to Cheshire Cat levels. "Anyone here ever been on a stakeout?"

CHAPTER 33

From the branch below, Liza, who had spent the last half an hour messing around on her phone, glared up at us. "Could you guys stop eating for *five seconds*?" she snapped. "We're supposed to be keeping our eyes peeled for a psycho serial arsonist, not OD'ing on sugar, gluten, and trans fats."

"We *got* our eyes peeled," Ernie clapped back. "We just happen to have peeled a few candy bars, too."

I had to give the dude daps for that. I mean, it *was* pretty funny.

Down below, Liza sighed and went back to her phone.

"Hey, what are you playing?" I asked. "Minecraft? Because I'm having trouble finding a dragon egg and I could use a few tips."

"I'm not *playing* anything," Liza grumbled. "It's just . . . it's the *weirdest* thing." Frowning, she held her phone up so we could see the screen. "What do you guys see?"

The older one, I kind of recognized. I was pretty sure I'd seen her around town. The younger one, I recognized for sure; she was Emilia Peterson—the girl who, according to my grandpa, claimed to have seen the haunted piñata way back when.

Ernie was pointing at the older one. "That's, uh, Ms. Redgrave, isn't it? The city engineer. She presented at our school a couple of times for career day, I think."

"That's her," Liza said.

I pointed at the other one. "And that's Emilia Peterson, right? Miguel's buddy."

Liza nodded. "Uh-huh. And a local science legend. Emilia won the state science fair ten years straight, starting in second grade. Her last project was totally genius, too, almost like a real-life Gundam or Iron Man suit. That was her dream—to build giant, people-powered mechs just like she'd seen in all those anime cartoons growing up."

"Yeah, I heard she was pretty smart," I said. "My abuelo still remembers her."

"So check it out," continued Liza, "my working hypothesis is that most copycat criminals are totally obsessed with the backstory of the particular crimes they copycat. So I figured the more I learned about the Blackbriar legend, the more I'd learn about whoever's behind the fires—or at least, what they might be planning. My original idea was to interview all the people that were closest to Miguel. I figured that would give me the most insight into everything that had happened. But the deeper I dug, it only confirmed what the legend always claimed: that all the people closest to him—every single person who had given eyewitness testimony claiming to have seen the haunted piñata in the weeks following the tragedy—had vanished. That wasn't made up. I couldn't find even a single scrap of recent info on any of them. No current addresses. No phone numbers. No work information. Nada. It's like they all turned into ghosts."

"You're starting to believe the legend now, too, huh?" Ernie told her in a tone that said, *It's about time . . .*

"No, I'm not starting to believe the legend," Liza snapped. "My point is, of all the eyewitnesses, the one I wanted to interview most was Emilia, seeing as we both share a passion for the scientific. And I figured with her being the youngest, I'd have a pretty good chance of tracking her down. I assumed she'd be a research scientist for a major corporation or something. So I was more than a little surprised when she came up a dead end, too." Liza shrugged. "And that's about when I started noticing the resemblance between Emilia and Veronica Redgrave. I don't know... the whole thing just strikes me as odd."

It must've struck Carter as odd, too, because he started looking sort of worried. That is, as worried as a seven-foot-tall bloodsucking monster can look. "You think dat they relatives or sumthin'?"

"That's the weird part," said Liza. "There's really no connection between them. No family members, nothing. But *wow*, they look alike, don't they?"

They did. They really did. It was almost creepy in a way. "What do you think's going on, Liza?"

She gave another little shrug. "I honestly don't know."

CHAPTER 34

A few minutes later, Carter went off to "water" some shrubs (having just sucked down a two-liter bottle of Cherry Coke in a single gut-busting slurp!), and the three of us watched him scamper lightly across the park, silent as a shadow, before disappearing into a row of thick trees.

I had just opened my mouth to call "next"—I was already feeling the fizzy pressure of downing my fifth can of Mountain Dew—when a black van suddenly screeched to a stop at the curb, no more than fifteen yards away.

Almost before its wheels had stopped spinning, the side door flew open and out jumped three peeps in black clothes, black gloves, and black ski masks.

Coming straight for us.

I realized Liza was staring at her phone. *Again.* "Yo, put that away!" I hissed. "We got company! Check these dweebs out."

"I did check them out," Liza replied calmly. "And that's why I'm checking my messages. About twenty minutes ago, I decided to text the fire chief and let him know what we were up to, in case we got into any trouble. He hasn't texted me back, but right now I'm feeling pleased as a peach with my decision."

"How come?" Ernie asked.

Pocketing her phone, Liza said, "Because it looks like we just found some. Trouble, that is." Then, hopping down from the tree, she whispered, "*Run!*"

You didn't have to tell Ernie and me twice. We hopped down after her, hitting the ground running.

Now, I'll admit it: black clothes, black ski masks, bike chains? Yeah, not usually a friendly combination. But just to make sure that we weren't being overly paranoid, I glanced back to see whether we were *actually* being chased.

And guess what?

We *were* actually being chased!

Yep. Definitely not how I'd envisioned my night going.

Up ahead, the street was straight-up deserted—no traffic on the road, no foot traffic on the sidewalks. Still, we hauled nachas toward the light of the shops and the bright yellow glow of the streetlamps, all of us screaming: "CARTER! CARTER, WHERE ARE YOU? HELP!"

Because if he didn't find us, and fast . . .

As we darted into the tight gap between a bakery and a dry cleaner, Ernie shouted, "WHO ARE THOSE PEOPLE?!"

I shouted, "NO IDEA! MAYBE YOU SHOULD STOP AND ASK THEM!"

We half ran, half bumbled down one alleyway, then another, our sneakers pounding on the pavement and our hearts pounding in our chests. But as we came flying around the next corner, all three of us had to slam on the brakes! *Hard!*

Why, you ask?

Because we didn't have a choice!

We'd run straight into a *dead end!*

CHAPTER 35

Heavy footsteps echoed in the dark.

Gasping, choking on fear and dumpster stink, I whirled around in time to see one of the ski-mask-wearing baddies come running into view.

My stomach might have crawled into my throat. I *may* have locked arms with Ernie and shrieked like a terrified billy goat. But nobody can prove either of those things.

The goon stalked toward us, each step reverberating in my ears like cannon fire. The silvery moonlight reflected in his dark eyes and off the length of bike chain in his hand, and suddenly the alley didn't seem big enough for the four of us.

But the creepiest part? He didn't say anything! Not a single word! Just kept creeping closer and closer . . .

"Spread out!" Liza said, shoving Ernie and me away. "He can't catch us all!"

"No, but the one he catches, he's probably going to *hurt*!" I couldn't help pointing out.

"Exactly!" Ernie agreed. "Which means I got roughly a sixty-two percent chance of being murdered in some dark, dank back alley!"

"Dude, you're one out of three," I said. "You only have a *thirty-three* percent chance of being murdered in some dark, dank back alley."

"Not with my luck!"

"Guys, new plan!" Liza whispered, jerking us close

again. "My karate class has a kata designed *specifically* for when you're facing larger attackers. I think we can do this!"

"How does it go?" I shouted.

And Liza demonstrated, calling out the techniques as she did. "Hi-ya punch! Crescent kick! Tiger's mouth strike! Two-finger spear! Spinning backfist! Head of the crane! High kick! Sweep!"

When she finished, Ernie and I just gaped at each other. "Did you get any of that?" he asked me.

"Nah, she lost me at spinning backflip."

"It's a spinning back*fist!*" Liza snapped. "It's a punch, not gymnastics!"

"Well, you might want to stop explaining and start demonstrating," I said as another ski mask baddie appeared, melting out of the shadows at the mouth of the alley, "because the villains seem to be multiplying!"

The closest one snapped the bike chain between his big black-gloved hands. Gulp. Then he ground it against the brick wall, scraping up sparks. Double gulp.

A heartbeat later, just as Ernie let out a shriek that could've raised the dead—

"His technique lacks a little finesse," Liza said. "But it works."

Ernie shouted, "CARTER!" and we all rushed breathlessly over, throwing our arms around vampire Bruce Lee.

"What took you so long?" I teased, beaming up at him.

His face split into a fangy grin. "Sorry. I *really* had to pee."

"If you would've peed any longer," I said, "the three of us would've probably ended up peeing our pants!"

Then—*Ping! Ping!*

Something struck the wall just above Carter's head.

Ping! Ping! Ping!

Three more somethings struck almost the exact same spot.

I whirled around. Charging toward us, maybe half a football field away, was another ski mask goon. Which was obviously bad news . . . but there was even *worse* news!

In his gloved hands, winking wickedly in the moonlight, was some kind of weapon. A tranquilizer dart gun! I'd watched enough movies from the Jurassic Park franchise to be absolutely positive.

In other words—

"¡CORRAN!" I screamed. *"Go, go!"*

We ran. Carter led the way out of that alley and down another. We raced through a dizzy maze of dumpsters and crates, barred-up back doors, and broken-down boxes, until the sound of chasing footsteps faded into the silent night, and all I could hear was my own pounding heart.

As we came spilling out behind the strip mall, I shouted, "Liza, hurry! Call the police! Let's get these bozos a nice shiny pair of handcuffs to go with the bike chains!"

But then I realized Liza wasn't there.

She wasn't anywhere!

And neither was Ernie!

"CARTER—WHERE'D THEY GO?!" I screeched.

The answer was pretty obvious, though: Liza and Ernie had gone one way, Carter and I another!

The chupacabra looked shook, like he'd just watched a magician pull a rabbit out of thin air. "¡No sé, Jorge!"

We barely had time to rush back into the alleyway, searching for our missing compadres, when a low crackling sound made us trade "What now?" glances.

We backed slowly out of the alley, looking curiously around—and guess what we saw?

CHAPTER 36

It was another ski mask baddie! This one was in a black hoodie and construction boots.

So there are four of these creeps in total, I thought, *not three.*

For a frozen moment Carter and I just stood there, staring dazedly at the masked villain while he just squatted there, staring back at us.

Then the whole crazy situation puzzled itself together in my brain and I said—as it slowly dawned on me—"He's the arsonist . . . they *all* are. They must be an arsonist *gang!*"

But no sooner had I opened my mouth to shout "Let's get 'em!" than Mr. Matchstick Brain, probably sensing something like that was coming, leapt to his feet, dug a small glass vial out of his pocket, and tossed it into the smoking tinder.

The vial burst. Its contents mixed with the fire and suddenly a wall of bright green flames—¡Dios mío! Like a boiling tsunami!—exploded upward, licking and leaping hungrily up the wall!

Carter and I barely made it five steps before a wave of hot air struck us like a huge invisible bedsheet, and we had to throw up our hands to shield our faces.

Smoke billowed. The spreading flames sizzled and burned, stretching across the alleyway like greedy reaching fingers.

There was no way past it. None!

Unless, of course, we were itching to look like one of those oh-so-yummy lemon-butter chickens you see dripping deliciousness on supermarket rotisseries . . . (PS: we *weren't*.)

Through the dancing curtains of flames, I could see the arsonist making his getaway, the sound of his pounding footsteps echoing fainter and fainter. Next thing I knew, he met up with a couple of his buddies way down at the far end of the alley (the two losers Carter had clobbered, it looked like), and then all three of them disappeared, swallowed by shadows.

"Dang it!" I shouted. "We almost had him!"

Just then, Liza and Ernie appeared out of nowhere, spilling out of the next alleyway over. They were both panting, wild-eyed, and sweating like Squidward at the neighborhood fish fry.

"WHERE'D YOU GUYS GO?!" I yelled at them.

"WHERE'D *YOU* GUYS GO?!" they yelled back.

Ernie's panicked eyes flew to the wall of poison-green flames. "HAUNTED PIÑATA MAGIC!" he shrieked.

"Nope! Just plain old arson!" I said. "Courtesy of the ski mask goons!"

But E-dog wasn't listening. "Oh, no! That's Mr. Sweet's candy shop!" he cried, nearly tripping over a fire hydrant. "That's my favorite candy shop in the entire world!"

I turned to Liza. "Liza, dial nine-one-one!"

"¡No hay tiempo!" shouted Carter, and I realized he was right—there wasn't any time! The fire station was at least fifteen minutes away, which meant that all the firefighters were at least fifteen minutes away, which, judging by the intensity of the fire, meant that this entire building—maybe even this entire block!—would be nothing more than a pile of smoldering ash *long* before any of the bomberos had even hooked their hoses to the fire hydrant.

Fire hydrant.

FIRE HYDRANT!

"That's it!" I screamed.

Liza looked confused. "*What's* it?!"

"¡Ayúdenme!" I cried, rushing over to the little yellow hydrant. "Help me!"

Ernie and Liza caught on pretty fast. They hustled over, and together we strained and pulled, twisting, gripping, our muscles screaming, the skin of our palms burning—

But the stupid hydrant's stupid spinning thingamajig wouldn't budge!

Meanwhile, Carter—who probably didn't have much experience with fire hydrants—just sort of watched us like, *Whatcha doin'?*

"Do either of you happen to own a giant wrench?" I shouted.

"Oh, sure!" Liza shouted back. "But I think I left it in my other shorts!"

"If only Superman was here!" Ernie cried, basically reading my mind.

And then—*eureka!*

"Dude, forget Superman!" I said. "We got SUPA-CARTER!"

I whirled around and gave the big guy a quick anatomy lesson on fire hydrants. Only at first, he was all like—

A split second later, there was this ginormous *WHOOSH!* and a geyser of freezing cold water shot out of the fire hydrant as if shot out of a . . . well, a fire hydrant.

Water met fire. They didn't seem to like each other. A mushroom cloud of steam billowed skyward, mixing with the smoke, and the flames instantly died down.

"SHEEEOOOWWW!" I cheered as the four of us started jumping up and down, smacking hands and hugging each other. The score was now HOME TEAM—ONE. EVIL, ARSONIST JERKS—BIG FAT ZERO!

Yeah, we were totally fired up! (See what I did there?) I mean, thanks to us, those fire-starting zonzos had just seen their evil plans go up in smoke! (Sorry, can't help myself.)

Right then, a white sedan with BOCA FALLS FIRE DE-PARTMENT painted on it pulled up alongside us. The door swung open, and out climbed the tall, muscular figure of Kenneth the fire chief.

"I got your message," he said, looking all sweaty and frazzled. "What happened here?"

So we told him everything. How the arsonists had

tried to kidnap us, and how we'd totally shut down their latest attempt at a five-alarm fire.

I watched the chief's face change from concern to relief to borderline annoyance as he listened. When we finished, he said, "You didn't recognize any of them? You don't have any idea who they might be?"

We all shook our heads (including Carter—who, by the way, was *supposed* to be pretending to be my loyal, *non*-English-speaking pooch). But then a thought struck me—struck me like a thunderbolt!

Oh my gosh . . .

"It was Zane!" I suddenly shouted. "Zane and his soccer minions!"

CHAPTER 37

The gasp Liza gave could've probably been heard all the way from my old El Sereno neighborhood back in East L.A. "Jorge, are you positive?!"

"I'm not *positive* positive," I said. "But think about it—there's a whole gang of them, about the same number as Zane's main crew. And they're all pretty big. Heck, that's probably why none of them said anything to us! So we wouldn't recognize their voices! Oh, and don't forget Zane's big threat in the cafeteria!"

Liza gave me a look like, *That's not exactly an airtight case there, my guy,* but Ernie was snacking what I was packing.

"Hey, I think Jorge is right!" he said excitedly. "Zane's the biggest jerk in school, and you've got to be a pretty big jerk to try to burn down Mr. Sweet's. The logic checks out!"

The fire chief, meanwhile, just stood there watching us for several seconds in silent concentration. Finally he said, "All right, head over to the station. I'll need statements from all of you. I'm going to put a report together, especially if you're planning on making any serious accusations. I'll meet you there in a few minutes. Have a stop to make first." As he climbed back into his car, his phone buzzed and he answered it, saying, "Yes, on my way. Everything's fine. The situation is under control." Then he started the car and, looking out the window at us, said, "Go straight to the firehouse and wait for me there."

No big surprise, the four of us were all buzzing with excitement as we started up the road toward the station house. I mean, we'd cracked—okay, *almost* cracked—a forty-year-old town mystery! Sure, the arsonists had gotten away. But at least now we'd proven that there *were* arsonists—a whole gang of them, in fact—and that it wasn't some übercreepy haunted piñata monster rampaging around town, "turning up the heat" on everyone.

Honestly, I was just relieved. Relieved that my

grandma was still the scariest thing in Boca Falls, and relieved that two of my best friends weren't going to have to move away after all. The arsonists' reign of terror was officially over. Now that we'd pulled the curtain back on them, people weren't just going to hide in their houses anymore, all afraid of some candy-stuffed fairy tale. And because those fire-starting tontos had lost their power to scare people, they'd basically lost their power to control them. Because that's all fear is—just another way to control people.

The night was cool and getting cooler by the time we reached the fire station.

Clearly nobody was home, but we jogged up the steps anyway, and were swinging open the main door when a buzzing, whirring sound made us turn and look up.

It was a sleek black delivery drone. One of Mr. Rathbone's—delivering the late-night edition of the newspaper to the firehouse.

Or should I say, it was *attempting* to deliver the late-night edition, because the actual *delivering* part never quite happened.

"Don't worry!" Carter exclaimed, leaping up to

grab the drone and Hulk-smashing it to bits on the firehouse steps. "I killed it!"

He wasn't kidding. All the king's horses and all the king's men couldn't have put Mr. Delivery Drone back together again. Hopefully Mr. Rathbone's insurance policy covered "acts of chupacabras." I doubted it, though.

"Dude, what'd you do that for?" Ernie burst out.

Carter's eyes bugged like they were looking to permanently relocate from his face. "*Wat*? You wanna get STUNG?! Dat one of those new species of giant metal mosquitos I been seeing lately! These things *MEAN*!"

Then he raised a giant furry foot and brought it down *hard*, crushing the drone's big propeller thingy. There was an electric *zap!* and then a puff of smoke, and that was pretty much the ball game.

"I FINALLEE CAUGHT ONE!" Carter cheered. *"Sheeeeeow!"*

"Carter, that wasn't a mosquito!" I tried to explain. "It's a newspaper delivery drone! That's private property!"

But the chupacabra just shrugged like, *So what?* "Well, somebody better tell Mr. Private to teach his property not to sneak up on people like that. Is not polite."

Liza, meanwhile, hadn't been paying much attention to any of this. Her gaze was focused—I'm talking Superman X-ray-vision-level focused—on the newspaper that had dropped from the drone's wire basket. Now her hands snatched it up and her eyes rapidly scanned the front page as a big fat question mark seemed to etch itself deeper and deeper into the center of her forehead.

We all quickly gathered round. "Hey, what's up?" I asked.

"Check this out!" Liza shouted.

Carter looked shocked. "Dat's tomorrow's newspaper!"

Ernie looked even more shocked. "Oh, no! We were too late!" Then his eyebrows knit together in confusion. "Wait. No. We were too *EARLY*!"

"Hol' up. Were we too late or too early?" Carter sounded equally lost. "My mind a little confused . . ."

"Listen to this!" Liza said, and began reading the article out loud: "'Three local youths and their peculiar-looking dog were unfortunately believed to have been trapped in the flames.'" She looked straight at me now. "Guys, do you realize what this means?"

"OMG, *YES!*" shrieked Ernie. "It means we were caught in the fire! It means . . . it means we're *GHOSTS!*"

If Liza's eyeballs had hands, they would've reared back and smacked Ernie upside the head. *Hard.* "We're not *ghosts*, Ernie! And we weren't caught in any fire. No, it means something far more sinister."

I knew what it meant, too. I knew because it had just dawned on me.

"We're . . . undead ghouls?" Ernie tried.

Definitely not what it meant.

"No, it's *Mr. Rathbone*," Liza said ominously. "It's been him all along!"

What she said.

CHAPTER 38

It was about time we broke our own news for a change. So here it was, courtesy of my overactive imagination—

EXTRA! EXTRA! READ ALL ABOUT IT!

Mr. Raymond Rathbone the fire starter! Boca Falls' favorite newspaperman is the mastermind behind the last forty years of fiery terror! Local heroes foil his best-laid plans, outsmarting his four ski-mask-wearing henchmen and winning the key to the city!

Pretty catchy, if I do say so myself. But also pretty true. His own front page had basically proved as much. I mean, how else could he have written a story about a fire that hadn't happened yet, and *didn't* happen because we'd been there to stop it?

Answer: he couldn't have. Not unless he knew

about it beforehand, had schemed it up with his gang of masked henchmen, and wrote the article in advance.

In fact, wasn't that the *Tribune*'s slogan? "Mañana's News, Today"? Guess it was more than just a catchy motto.

But the best part of it all? By the time his buddies had let him know that their latest scheme had gone up in—well, *flames*, it had been too late to recall his army of delivery drones, which meant that these papers were lying on front steps and porches all over Boca by now! *Whoops.*

I could practically hear the evil matchstick head now, sounding like every villain in every cartoon *ever*: "And I would've gotten away with it, too, if it hadn't been for you meddling kids!"

Anyway, the four of us were practically jumping out of our socks, we were so amped! We couldn't wait to tell the fire chief. But when he didn't show for ten whole minutes (which felt more like ten whole *lifetimes*), we started to get a little antsy. And that's when we came across something *very* interesante . . .

"Guys, I think dis is bad," Carter said, picking up a small note from the fire chief's desk.

"What does it say?" asked Liza.

Carter shrugged. "Dunno. Can't read."

But as usual, the big guy's animal instincts were spot-on.

The handwritten note, scrawled in neat cursive on firehouse stationary, read:

Raymond Rathbone says he needs to see you asap!
Waiting for you at the Blackbriar mansion. Says he
might know something about the recent string of fires.
Received 8:47 p.m.

"That note's from less than half an hour ago!" Liza shrieked, checking the time on her phone. "The chief is walking straight into a trap!"

She wasn't kidding, either. It was a straight-up *ambush*! "The mansion's probably the headquarters for Raymond and his matchstick buddies!" I shouted. "Their evil bad guy lair! They're probably all there right now, waiting for the fire chief!"

Meanwhile, all the blood had gone out of Ernie's face, and for a moment there it looked like he might've turned into an undead ghoul after all.

"What are we gonna do?" he squeaked.

"We have to get over there and warn him," said Liza. "And fast!"

But E-dog was already shaking his head, not liking the sound of that. "Actually, I was thinking something a little less hands-on and *a lot* less dangerous."

"Well, think again!" I said, grabbing him by the shirtsleeve. "¡Vámonos!"

And, naturally, at moments such as these, it was time for—

AN ULTRACOOL HEROES-GEARING-UP-FOR-BATTLE MONTAGE!

Just kidding about the gearing-up thing. . . . Those fire suits are too big and heavy. We did grab a few flashlights, though.

CHAPTER 39

I'm not even going to try to sugarcoat it: the old Black-briar mansion up on Mount Vista Grande was just about the creepiest crib on the entire planeta.

As a matter of fact, on a standard creepiness scale of one to ten, this place would've easily registered a fifteen! And that was in full sunshine and underneath a sky full of *My Little Pony* rainbows. Never mind at the dead of night, with no moon or stars, and swarms of fruit bats screeching through the spindly trees, beady eyes flashing.

The best part, though? The four of us were about to try to sneak our way *inside* that happy house of horrors. Fun, huh?

Now, you'd think that busting into the abandoned, run-down, doppelganger of a haunted fairy-tale castle would be easy-peasy. Think again.

The gate had been opened, but the place itself was sealed up tighter than the treasure room in Fort Knox. All the obvious ways in—say, places where pieces of wall had burned down or crumbled away—were fenced off by barbed wire, and all the doors all the way around were securely hinged and even more securely locked. Yeah, we tried all twenty-five of them.

And if things weren't bad enough already, as we

were sneaking around the eerie, abandoned, over-grown gardens out back, one of us spotted a squirrel chillaxing under a half-dead oak tree.

I'll let you guess which one of us it was . . .

"Carter, get *back* here!" I shouted as he bolted off into the night after it.

"*Carter!*" Liza hissed.

"Dude?" I heard Ernie rasp.

We caught up with the runaway bloodsucker by the southeast wing of the old manor, and when we found him, he was buried up to his waist in a clump of oily black bushes that appeared to be growing out of the crumbly stonework. Above him, strung with coils of rusty barbed wire, was a busted window.

"Bro, you can't go running off like that!" I quietly scolded him. "You'll totally blow our cover!"

"Sorry," Carter whispered. "You know how I get around ardillitas."

"Carter, get out of there already!" Liza snapped. "And stop wasting time! We've got to find a way into this place!"

"Already did!" the chupacabra happily an-nounced, still buried in the bushes.

We all blinked. "Huh?"

"The squirrel showed me! He ran in here. ¡Mira!"

We all stuck our heads into the bush. About two feet in, butted up against the side of the manor, I spotted something like cellar doors (minus one of the doors). And beyond it, spiraling down into the earth, a set of shadowy stony steps.

"Uh, can anyone say *creepy*?" whispered Ernie.

CHAPTER 40

Surprise, surprise, the Blackbriar mansion was just as much a Halloween Horror Nights on the inside as it was on the outside. There were these thick, sticky cobwebs hanging from ceilings, scraggly vines growing up the walls, hordes of Chihuahua-size rats playing hide-and-seek in the corners, and a smorgasbord of other creepy-crawlies creeping and crawling between every crack and gap and cavity in the broken floorboards.

Basically, you name it, this place had it.

"Doesn't look like anyone's home," I whispered, stepping carefully over a collapsed ceiling beam, which—creepily enough—sort of resembled the bony remains of a dead cat.

Up ahead, Carter was channeling his inner

bloodhound—head back, snout up, sniffing curiously at the heavy, moldy air. Suddenly, his mismatched eyes sharpened and the fur rose coarse and thick along his spine.

"What is it?" I whispered. "What do you smell?"

"*Evil*," answered the chupacabra, and I, of course, immediately regretted asking the question.

Meanwhile, Ernie—who had obviously also heard Carter's not-so-cheery assessment—gave a gulp loud enough to raise the dead. "Okay, so am I the only one who thinks we should probably head back home now?"

"Yes. Now, shush and c'mon!" rasped Liza, motioning for us to follow.

The floorboards squeaked and dust clouds bloomed under our sneakers as we crept down a long, spooky hallway. Every inch of this place, it looked like—every inch of the walls, every inch of the ceilings—was scarred by burn marks, blackened by fire.

The flames that had swept through here long ago had warped everything they'd touched, from the silver sconces high on the walls, to the windowpanes, to

the door handles and outlet plates. The place reeked of destruction, of decay.

But it wasn't just what I could see or smell that put a tremble in my bones and a chill in my heart. There was something else, too. Something I couldn't quite put my finger on.

It was a sense. No, more like *a vibe*. Some creeping, sneaking, slithering sensation that seemed to scuttle across the dusty floorboards and over our sneakers and up the sides of our legs.

The place felt . . . alive.

Or maybe the right word was *haunted*.

A few moments later, we stepped through a set of wide double doors and into a room so big and cavernous that a dragon could've changed its name to Smaug and happily brooded over its treasure here. Swirls of black-gray ash covered everything—and I do mean *everything*. If I didn't know better, you could've told me that Mount Vesuvius had erupted somewhere in the vicinity, and it would've been hard not to believe you. I didn't see much furniture, just the charred remains of a once-ginormous banquet table and what might've been a massive wardrobe now draped with a big tarp.

"This is where it all started . . ." whispered Liza, her eyes wide and glittering in the glow of her flashlight.

"Where what all started?" I whispered back.

"The legend of the haunted piñata." She shone her linterna around, the beam picking up crumbling, vine-covered columns and cracked, checkerboard marble floors. "Yeah, this has to be the grand ballroom. The place where Miguel Valdez Blackbriar had his big birthday bash, and where all the kids sang and mocked him."

As she spoke, goose bumps broke out all over my legs and arms, and I could almost see the scene playing out in my head.

"Yep," Liza went on, "this is the very room where the fire started and the legend was born."

"You keep talking all ominous like that," I admitted, "and I'm going to pee my pants."

"I already peed mine un poquito," Carter said.

Creeping up behind Liza, Ernie said, "I just don't get it. If Rathbone really *is* behind the fires, then how do you explain all the haunted piñata sightings? I mean, people claim to have seen that thing for *years*. Even Jorge thought he saw it!"

And Liza, now down on one knee, peeking underneath the big blue tarp, said, "I think I can explain that," and suddenly, she yanked the tarp back like a magician revealing her greatest trick.

And the moment I saw what had been hidden underneath (which, spoiler alert, *wasn't* a giant wooden dresser), I nearly swallowed my own tongue!

Because what was actually under there was a . . . a . . . *how should I put this*?

Oh, just see for yourself!

CHAPTER 41

It was sort of hard to describe the thing. The simplest way, I guess, was if Godzilla and Optimus Prime had a baby, *that* would be it.

And even though it looked almost exactly like the terrifying creature I'd seen that night in the woods, I couldn't say for sure with one hundred percent certainty that it *actually* was.

There was just something *different* about it. Super weird, I know.

Crouching to examine the steel underbelly of the bot, Ernie rasped, "It's a hundred percent ghost-free! No sugary ectoplasmic guts whatsoever!" Then he leaned over and sniffed the thing's rear end. "It's *gasoline* powered!"

Carter was also sniffing the piñata bot's heinie. The two of them looked like a couple of frisky pooches at the neighborhood dog park. "And look at da feet! Da bottoms! Dey look like Rollerblades!"

Liza and I stared at each other with eyes so wide that it was a wonder they didn't pop out of our faces and fist-bump one another.

"The tracks we saw in the woods!" I shouted. "Those deep, straight, rut-like tracks!"

"Jorge, that means you *didn't* imagine seeing the haunted piñata, after all!" she whispered, sounding somewhere between relief and mind-numbing horror. "And neither did anyone else who claimed to have seen the monster! Like Ms. Blanco. Or the Blackbriars' servants and family. They actually saw it! Well, at least what they *thought* was it."

All of a sudden, there came a slow, steady clapping sound from somewhere in the shadows.

The four of us whirled around, eyes scanning the gloom, as a figure melted out of the dark. Needless to say, we all knew who it was even before we saw his grinning, villain-y face.

"Bravo, bravo, my little sleuths! Sherlock Holmes would be very proud!"

CHAPTER 42

It was Raymond Rathbone!

Boca Falls' very own newspaper-printing Lex Luthor!

And even though I wasn't exactly surprised to see him, I'd be lying if I said my heart didn't skip a beat.

Okay, more like *fifty* beats.

His smooth, hairless head gleamed white in the glow of Liza's flashlight as he shook it at us.

"If only my beat reporters had half the nose for a good story as you three, our circulation would be nationwide by now!"

In his gloved hand, he held some kind of tiny remote controller.

Now his thumb played with a tiny joystick, there was a whirling sound above us, and—

My first instinct was to scream. Which I did. And loud, too.

My second instinct was to look up as my panicking brain tried frantically to figure out where in the fajitas that ginormous version of the basket from the board game Mouse Trap had dropped from. Which I also did.

Squinting, I could just make out a network of steel tracks running along the vaulted ceiling. Rathbone must've been moving the cage thingy along those tracks as he lined it up for the big drop on Carter.

Like one of those claw-hand arcade machines! I thought, kind of impressed and kind of panicking.

Carter, for his part, was none too pleased. He hissed and growled, slashing uselessly at the thick metal bars as Rathbone stood watching him with a vicious glint in his eyes.

"My apologies," said the cage-dropping scoundrel cheerily, "but pets indoors have always been—if you'll pardon the pun—a *pet peeve* of mine. Do you have any idea how difficult is to get fur out of a linen couch?"

I didn't. And I didn't care.

"Hey, let 'im go!" Ernie demanded.

But Rathbone, the jerk he was, clearly wasn't in an obliging mood. Instead he clicked another button, and this time there was a huge reverberating *bang!* as thick steel shutters crashed down all around us, blocking every window, every door, every stinkin' way out of this place!

"Hey, let us *go*!" Ernie shrieked.

Unfortunately, that didn't work either.

"Let you go?" Rathbone echoed mockingly. "But

you've only just arrived!" With a grin about as friendly as a bear trap, he raised his arms and gestured grandly around the room. "Welcome to Blackbriar Manor! Once the most beautiful home in all the southwestern United States! And, ironically enough, the last home any of you will ever step foot inside."

Pinched underneath his left arm was a folded-up newspaper. He chucked it, Frisbee-style, at our feet, and as it flopped open, I saw that it was the same late edition we'd seen back at the firehouse.

"Hot off the presses!" Rathbone's voice boomed with a sickening blend of triumph and pride. "Quite the headline, don't you agree? Arguably my finest bulldog edition ever!"

"Too bad it's fake news, Rathbone," Liza butted in. "We stopped the fire, and here we are, still breathing."

Somehow the evil magnate's grin became even more vicious. "For *the moment*, at least . . ."

Suddenly my mind flashed on the fire chief. He was around here. Somewhere! His car had been parked right out front, which meant that bitcoins to doughnuts, he was probably sneaking around the mansion at this very moment, getting ready to make his move! And just like that, I knew what I had to do: buy the dude some time!

"Hate to sound all 1950s Batman, Rathbone," I said, "but you won't get away with this. My grandma is going to come looking for me!" Then, pausing for a second to consider the chances of that actually happening: "Eh, who am I kidding? She isn't going to come looking for me. But *their* parents will!"

"Yeah, you're not gonna get away with this, you creep!" Ernie shouted.

Rathbone laughed, and it was a textbook evil-villain laugh, too—a total *muhahahaha*! Apparently bad guys actually laugh like that in real life. Wild, I know. "Ah, but I will. You see, thanks to all my years in the newspaper racket, I learned the most important rule in the biz: It pays to have friends. Lots and *lots* of friends."

An instant later, four more figures melted out of the shadows. Figures we'd recently seen. *Very* recently, as a matter of fact.

THE SKI MASK BADDIES!

I had a split second to wonder, *Who the heck are those creeps?* Then it was show-and-tell time, and oh boy, what a show it was . . .

CHAPTER 43

"But I don't get it!" I burst out, still pointing, real accusingly, at the baron. "You—you burned down your *own bank*?!"

"A smokescreen," he replied smugly. "An unfortunate sacrifice necessary to throw off suspicion."

Guess it worked, too. The fire had definitely thrown us for a loop.

Ernie, meanwhile, was looking like a real-life shocked emoji with his eyes bugging halfway out of his sweat-slicked face. "Wait up," he gasped, "so not only is the owner of the town newspaper in on this, but the town banker *and* the town engineer are, too?! This is *bananas!*"

He wasn't kidding. The whole thing *was* bananas. Banana splits, in fact! But then came the cherry on top: the next thing I knew, three of Veronica Redgrave's slim fingers disappeared into her mouth and—ugh, *gross!*—she pulled out her teeth!

Wait, no. Not her teeth!

More like dentures!

Still gross, though.

And she wasn't done yet. Next, off came those epic eyebrows. She just peeled the pair of giant caterpillars right off her face as if they were hairy Band-Aids!

And without the fake teeth and fake eyebrows, she looked pretty much *exactly* like the girl in that old yearbook picture! Just older, of course.

"Oh my gosh!" Ernie cried. "She looks even *more* like Emilia Peterson than before! It's almost like they're the same person!"

"Not almost," corrected Liza. "They *are* the same person." Then, turning her attention back to Veronica—or should I say, *Emilia*—Liza said: "I should've known you were involved the second I saw that bot!"

"My, they *are* brainy." said Emilia, her real eyebrows now raised in surprise. I noticed she was carrying a small steel cage. Little white lab mice skittered and squeaked inside. And as she loaded the cage into a hatch in the side of the piñata bot, it finally dawned on me:

"That's why we found all those mice by the butcher shop," I said aloud.

Emilia smirked, patting the cage almost lovingly. "Precisely. The mice are my canaries in the coal mine, if you will. Allow me to explain. The colorant we formulated—the substance we use to give our fires that *spectacular* haunting greenish hue—also contains a few other ingredients, which, when superheated, create a semi-deadly neurotoxin before dissolving into a thin, fairy dust–like mineralization.

Now, keep in mind that when our bot is operational, we run gas fires in the eye sockets, periodically adding in some of our compound to give its eyes that trademark blazing-green appearance. However, in a poorly ventilated space and in large concentrations, the compound can cause full body paralysis in most mammals inside of twenty minutes. Smaller mammals, such as lab mice, can only withstand its effects for about five minutes or so. In other words, when the mice begin going belly-up, I know it's time for me to take a breather."

Huh. So I guess that not only explained the mice, it also explained the glittery trails in the woods.

"Wait. You're saying you operate that piñata bot from *inside*?" Ernie asked, gazing wide-eyed up at the giant bot. "Like a full-on Iron Man suit?"

Then Emilia showed us her real teeth. They definitely fit her face better. "Pretty cool, isn't it?"

Wow, bad guys—er, in this case, bad *gals*—just love to toot their own horns, don't they?

"Super cool!" Ernie cheered. But the slam of Liza's elbow straight into his ribs had him changing his tune real quick. "I mean, that's super *boring*. You stink!"

Next moment, off came the third ski mask, and this time the curly gray hair and smiling gray eyes that stared smugly back at us nearly sent my eyebrows shooting through the roof!

It was ... it was ...

MS. BLANCO!

If a trio of giant flying pandas had flown in through one of the shuttered windows right then and started dancing the Macarena right in the middle of the ballroom, I don't think I could've been any more shocked.

And Ernie was right there with me. His jaw was practically scraping the scorched floorboards as he erupted, "*What? You're in on this, too, Ms. Blanco?!*"

"It was all right under our noses," I heard Liza murmur. "Everything we needed to crack the case was right there in the woods by my dad's shop."

"You five were pretty sloppy that day," I couldn't help pointing out. Yeah, I was going to take my pokes at them. Even if they were the last pokes I ever took.

Baron von Belcherstaub looked like he wanted to bite me, but he used his mouth to grin at me instead. "I could not agree more!" he exclaimed. "But keep in mind that her father's shop was only our second act of arson in the last six years, and one does have to—pardon the pun—warm up."

"Also, we were quite caught off guard by the panicked woman who came running out of the shop, screaming her head off," added Rathbone.

"Yes, we certainly had not expected her," said Emilia. "Our initial plan was to let the exterior security cameras catch a fleeting glimpse of our piñata bot. But, of course, the likelihood that she had already dialed someone for help made that too risky. We were forced to flee the scene. Fortunately, she fainted after seeing the bot and caused us no further trouble."

"But yes," continued the baron, "in our panic, we made several mistakes that day. However, I assure you that we're usually *much* more careful."

For the past few seconds, I'd noticed that Ms. Blanco's gray eyes had been laser-focused on Liza. At last, she spoke.

"You should know that I took little pleasure in burning down your family's shop," she said. "Your mother was more cordial to Miguel than most in Boca Falls, though I cannot say the same for your father. At any rate, it was not my favorite fire that I have ever started, and that is the honest truth."

"But I—I don't understand," whispered Liza, looking—and sounding—totally bewildered. "Your alibi was airtight. Lester the locksmith swore you'd been at his house at the time of the fire."

"Of course he did," Ms. Blanco replied matter-of-factly. "Because we've all sworn to protect each other."

Finally, off came the fourth and last ski mask, and well, yep . . .

There was Linus Lester. In all his smirking, creepy-teeth glory.

It was now official.

Mind.

Blown.

I mean, just think about it. The whole case had practically been served up to us on the world's shiniest silver platter.

The beads, pointing at Ms. B.

The matches, pointing at the banker baron.

The strange Rollerblade-like tracks, hinting at some giant bot, and clearly the work of a brilliant engineer, i.e., Emilia Peterson.

The petrified mice, pointing at the locksmith.

The ink-stained hanky, pointing at the newspaper guy.

Oh, and let's not forget the picked deadbolt I'd found in the butcher shop, once again *clearly* pointing at the sneaky, villainous locksmith.

The funny part was that we'd zeroed in on almost all the guilty parties pretty much from the jump. Only, we'd let ourselves get talked out of our suspicions, ironically enough, by the guilty parties themselves. Our fatal mistake was assuming there was just one villain. Epically embarrassing, I know. Kind of like when you correctly solve a math problem but accidentally write the wrong answer.

On the flip side, it *was* pretty good for our first case. Too bad we were all about to die, because I had a feeling that with some practice, we could've given Scooby-Doo and Mystery Inc. a run for their moolah.

"Aw, man, I can't take this!" Ernie burst out. "It's too much! I mean, is the *whole stinkin' town* in on it?!"

"Not the whole town," I said, slowly shutting my eyes as it finally hit me. "Just one more person."

CHAPTER 44

Ernie was really gaping now. It was a wonder his jaw was still attached to the rest of his head.

"*Who else?!*" he screeched.

"Dude, think about it," I told him. "We obviously walked into a trap. Check out that giant cage. In other words, they knew we were coming *long* before we actually got here."

Liza shook her head. "But how could they possibly have known that, Jorge?"

"Simple. Because *we* told them. Just like we told them about our stakeout. How else do you think they knew we were watching the shopping mall?"

"Hold up!" gasped Ernie. "Are you saying there's *a traitor* among us?" He turned, slowly, staring at each of us in turn. His voice shook with disbelief. "Is it . . . *you*, Carter?"

Carter gave Ernie a look like, *C'mon, bro, seriously?*

"It's not one of us," I explained. "It's the only other person we've been telling all our plans to. The same person who's been working against us from the beginning."

"Impressive," said a new voice. "Very, *very* impressive."

Then, like an evil genie materializing out of a bottle, the long athletic form of the fire chief melted out of deep shadow.

Gone was the smiling, friendly face we'd grown so accustomed to. In its place was a cold, calculating mask without the slightest trace of warmth or kindness. You could tell he'd quit playing the role of friendly neighborhood firefighter.

He said, "But obviously not quite smart enough to have seen the perfectly timed newspaper delivery and the letter on my desk for what they truly were— a trail of poisoned bread crumbs. Still, color me impressed."

I'd color you something else if I had a big enough crayon, I thought, clenching my hands into fists.

"The grand final twist!" Ernie burst out. "Can't believe I didn't see it coming! Captain Kirk totally would have!" He paused, turning back to the fire chief. "But *why*? Why team up with that bunch of losers?"

"Don't you get it?" Liza said. "They're probably all making bank. Every time the fires start, Rathbone's newspaper sales go through the roof; the baron's credit union starts handing out high-interest loans to 'help' people rebuild their burned-down property; Ms. Blanco's shop gets so packed you practically have to have an appointment; everyone's calling Linus's warehouse wanting new locks, upgraded security systems, whatever; and our beloved fire chief and city engineer make sure the whole twisted scheme goes undetected." Her voice was low and icy with anger. "The love of money really is the root of all evil, huh?"

"Ah, but that is where you are mistaken, pequeñita," said Ms. B. "It was never about the money."

"Yeah, right. Then what was it about?" I asked, making my best gimme-a-break face.

"*Revenge!*" sneered the baron. "Revenge on this wretched town, and revenge on its wretched people!"

When we all only stared, looking lost, Belcherstaub said, "The piñata bot. The fires. Isn't it rather obvious? For the last four decades, the six of us have devoted our lives to seeking vengeance for the horrific and needless death of Miguel Valdez Black-briar! I'm sure you are all familiar with the tragic tale. You have no doubt heard all about how those monstrous schoolmates of his plotted to utterly em-barrass Miguel on the celebration of the day of his birth. I'm sure you've heard all about their mocking songs, and their choreographed walkout, and the de-struction of Miguel's precious piñata—a special gift from Miguel's grandfather, the greatest piñata maker in all of Mexico. But you haven't heard the *whole* story. See, their vicious bullying did not drive poor Miguel into a wild rage. Quite the contrary. It drove him into a great, sinking sadness. The young boy was utterly heartbroken! So heartbroken, in fact, that he was un-able to pick himself up from the chair where he had sat to blow out his birthday candles. The candles, which, indeed, he never *did* blow out and which—as the legends claim—were the cause of the deadly fire."

Emilia Peterson, who looked like she was about to break down in tears, burst out with: "Miguel was a sweet soul! A strange and sheltered boy, certainly. But he did not deserve such a *wretched* fate! And nei-ther did his parents."

"However, it was not only the Blackbriars whose lives were destroyed that night," said Ms. B., picking up where the baron had left off. "See, in the days that followed certain individuals witnessed a miracle: Miguel's piñata came to life—alive with the spirit of poor Miguel! The individuals who saw the piñata took it as a glorious omen. A sign that the boy's spirit had lived on after the fiery tragedy. But when they began to spread the wonderful news around town, they were laughed at in scorn, called liars and lunatics, and slowly but surely expelled from society. The entire town turned against them. When they sought loans to rebuild the Blackbriar estate, the bank refused them. When they tried to raise money from the community, the newspaper ran disparaging stories suggesting that the funds would be better spent repairing the old sanitorium, that way these so-called piñata witnesses could check themselves into it. This, of course, was all little more than pretense.

"The truth was that the citizens of this godforsaken town could not bear to face the stain of their sins, and so they sought to erase all memory of the Blackbriars, and thereby of their own guilt. For I tell you that the parents of those wicked children who bullied and ridiculed poor Miguel are as responsible as their offspring. Because it was *those* malevolent parents, who, by murmuring in their homes about the Blackbriars day after day, made it easy for their children to hate him, and brought about the evil of that *cursed* night. In any event, the few who sought to preserve the legacy of the Blackbriars and had been driven out of town would soon band together. And together they would discover a higher purpose: to destroy the lives of those who had destroyed theirs and take their full revenge, for both Miguel and for themselves!"

And with those words, Ms. B. reached up and pulled off her wild, gray hair. Wait, no! She pulled off a *wig*!

Underneath, her real hair was a light reddish-brown, shorn close to her scalp. Then her glasses came off, and her contacts, and that large fluffy scarf she always wore around her neck—and just like that, I recognized her! Recognized the *real* her!

"Luna Thorne!" I shouted. The Blackbriars' maid!

CHAPTER 45

The grand ballroom of the Blackbriar mansion suddenly started looking an awful lot like the backstage of the Globe theater during intermission. Wigs flew off, makeup was smeared away, fake teeth and gums dropped into waiting hands, and prosthetic noses and chins and foreheads were peeled off, revealing— well, different noses and different chins and different foreheads.

In other words, the masks were finally coming off. Only, in this case, *literally*.

And there they stood—all the "missing people." Everyone close to the Blackbriars. Every single person who'd claimed to have seen the haunted piñata and who had vanished soon after.

But the most mind-blowing part? None of them

had *actually* gone missing. They'd all been right here in Boca Falls, in disguise!

"Man, this is more last-minute secret identity reveals than in a Spy Kids movie!" I shouted.

Ms. B.—or should I say, Ms. *Thorne*—said, "My real name is Luna, and I was the Blackbriars' maid for ten wonderful years. I was also the first to see the haunted piñata, the first to reach out to the people of Boca Falls, and the first to be treated like some kind of pariah. They said I was mad, depraved."

"And some of the vilest among this township even

said that this loving family whom I gladly served for most of my life had gotten what they deserved," added Raymond Rathbone. And like a flash I saw it— he was actually Reginald Stevens, the Blackbriars' butler!

Then I recognized the rest of them, too...

I'd seen all their pictures online and up on the wall in Liza's room. All their lives had gone up in flames the day the Blackbriar mansion had caught fire and so they'd come back for revenge, looking to set the rest of the town ablaze, too.

"I can't believe this," whispered Ernie. "It's like we're trapped in some kind of Nancy Drew nightmare!"

"Well, believe it," said Luna Thorne. And then, in typical gloating-movie-villain style, she gave us a rundown on how they'd pulled it all off. How they'd first secretly driven out the local banker and newspaper owners and established their own; how Emilia had built their secret weapon, the ultimate symbol of their revenge; how Reginald grew the gossip columns, amplifying the fear; how Jaxon unlocked any door that stood in their way; how the fire chief had made sure that none of them were ever suspected; and finally, how Luna herself had coordinated it all from her little bodega up on Main Street.

With eyes burning almost as fiercely as their piñata bot's, Luna went on with, "The real monsters in this town are its *citizens*! Not the haunted piñata, though we used the legend to drive fear into the hearts of these heartless people! To keep fresh in their minds the memory of their sins! And so, we have spent the last thirty-six years systemically targeting not only those who targeted us, but every person directly or indirectly responsible for the demise of the Blackbriars. And we will not stop until our vengeance is complete, and all of Boca Falls *burns* . . . burns like the Blackbriar mansion burned all those years ago!"

Geez, these peeps were taking the idea of holding a grudge to a whole other level! I'm not going to lie . . . it was pretty scary.

"Look," I said, "I get that you want to avenge Miguel, and that it was horrible what those kids did to him. No one should have to go through that, especially not on their birthday. But you can't destroy *an entire town* for something that happened forty years ago! There are innocent people living in Boca Falls. Like *me*! I'm not even from here, yo!"

"The *only* innocent was Miguel," said Benjamin Blackbriar darkly. "But not a single person in this forsaken town stood up for him. And now they will all pay!"

"But what about *ME*?" I shouted, feeling like they weren't really giving my situation a whole lot of consideration.

"You, unfortunately, are collateral damage," said Emilia coolly. "The three of you know too much. Thus, like an erroneous hypothesis, you must be discarded. But take some solace in the fact that no one in Boca has ever gotten closer to exposing us than you three. Not even Red Wilson. And he was one of this town's most decorated investigators."

Aha! So that's why they'd gone after Red. He must've come too close to putting the pieces together.

"Enough talk!" Rathbone—er, the Blackbriars' butler—snapped. "We have a mall to burn down and three kids and their mangy mutt to bury at the bottom of it."

Jaxon Randall's smiling beady eyes flicked from Reginald to us. And even without those awful fake teeth, the creep still had a grin that could've peeled paint. "You three putting out the candy shop fire might work out even better for us. You see, we've decided to take the piñata out to the mall and have Benjamin snap a few terrifying photographs for tomorrow's front page!"

Right then, the fire chief's hand disappeared into his coat and reappeared holding something small and sleek. Dios mío, it was a dart pistola! The same kind they'd been trying to tag us with earlier!

Fantástico . . .

I squeezed my eyes shut, preparing for a painful

sting, followed by a very long, very *deep* nap, when I heard, "HEY, YOU CAN'T DO DAT!"

I cracked open one eye.

It was Carter.

Carter had said that!

And I'm sure you can imagine the general reaction in the room . . .

There was a gasp heard around the world (well, at least around the ballroom), and as the six evil masterminds swung their shocked, gaping faces around to Carter, I honestly expected to see twelve eyeballs roll out of their sockets and plop stickily to the ground.

"Did that dog just talk?" screeched Emilia, stunned.

Jaxon gave a slow, confused blink. "I—I believe it did . . ."

"Look like we all got our secretos, huh?" replied the chupacabra with a sheepish grin. Then his bright eyes found mine and he whispered, "My plan was to keep quiet, so that at the perfect time I could surprise dem by sayin' sumthin'! Like jess now! See how surprised dey look? Now dey all confused and maybe dey forget about their evil plan!"

"We don't have time for any talking animals!"

snapped Luna Thorne. "Put the children to sleep and let's get ready to move!"

So much for forgetting their evil plan . . .

"Hold up!" I cried. "What about the talking dog? Heck, he's not even a dog! He's a *CHUPACABRA!*"

"Jorge is right!" Liza pitched in. "I mean, shouldn't we all just slow down and take a moment to discuss how the recent discovery of a previously-considered-make-believe species of bloodsucking omnivores reflects on our extremely limited knowledge of cryptozoology as a whole?"

"Maybe we can discuss over a bowl of goat-head soup?" suggested Carter, his stomach growling hungrily.

"As much as sweeping scientific inquiries interest me," said Emilia coldly, "we simply do not have the time for such a discussion. But now that we know it talks, we'll make sure to kill it, too."

Carter looked at me like, *Yikes!* "Maybe I shoulda kept my big boca shut, huh?"

The fire chief leveled the dart slinger on us again.

Liza, Ernie, and I all gulped again.

Grinning evilly, he said, "You play with fire, you get *burned.*"

BANG! An ear-busting, heart-stopping, courage-melting blast sounded, sending my stomach plummeting down to my toes.

And just when I thought it was all over (and this time for real), the entire wall behind us came crashing down as if struck by a ginormous wrecking ball.

We all ducked and crouched, arms covering our heads. Nobody had the slightest clue what had just gone down! But as the debris slowly settled, at least the "who" behind the "what" became crystal clear.

It was Red!

Aka BATHROBE RAMBO!

CHAPTER 46

"Did someone call for a *real* firefighter?" he said, sounding like some eighties action star making their big entrance.

"What an awesome line!" cried Ernie.

It was a pretty cool line. Also, a pretty cool entrance. But it wasn't time for high fives and Pepsis just yet.

"Mr. Wilson, they're the arsonists!" I shouted. "It's a *huge* conspiracy! They're all bad guys!"

Bathrobe Rambo nodded. "I know," he growled. "I heard everything."

Then he whirled around and—*clang!*—chopped the lock off Carter's cage with one big swing of his machete. The chupacabra scrambled out so fast he would've made Sonic the Hedgehog look like Sonic the *Sloth*, and the second he did, pretty much every single member of Team Arsonist drew dart slingers and let 'em rip.

A hail of tranquilizer darts came whizzing our way. The five of us dove for cover behind the charred remains of a baby grand piano, hearing the *thunk! thunk! thunk!* of the needle-tipped sleepy-makers burying themselves into the piano's wooden lid.

Gripping one of the dust-covered legs, I poked my head out just in time to see Emilia Peterson scuttle quickly up a hatch into the steel underbelly of the piñata bot.

An instant later, the huge glass eyes blazed to life, burning a bright poison green, and then—

WORST-CASE SCENARIO!

ROOOAAR

RESISTANCE SEEMS TOTALLY FUTILE RIGHT ABOUT NOW!

A wave of searing heat, like the world's hottest pizza oven, washed over us. Sweat instantly broke out all over me. Under my armpits. Behind my ears. Between my toes. Pretty much *everywhere!*

¡Dios mío! Suddenly I had a pretty good idea of what a rotisserie chicken must feel like. And no joke, I felt so bad for our flying feathered friends right then that I almost swore off roasted poultry. *For life!*

Red, who had been hunkered down next to me, suddenly lit the fuse of a fat, bright-red firecracker. Then he leapt to his feet and, rearing back like a legit MLB pitcher, chucked it in a high, whirling arc.

A moment later, there was a huge *BOOM!* and a shower of green and red sparkles lit up the ballroom, crackling and snapping all around us.

"Dude, THAT'S your weapon of choice?!" I shouted, staring down at the mess of sparklers, pop-pops, and mini rockets dangling from the loops of his combat vest.

Red shrugged. "I'm a pacifist. Plus, fireworks are cool."

A pacifist! ¡Órale!

"In the words of Spock, your armament selection is HIGHLY illogical!" Ernie yelled at him.

Suddenly, another wall of flame courtesy of Emilia's deadly creation roared toward us and over us, enveloping us in a fiery cocoon. The edges of the piano began to smolder. Through the baseboard, I heard a series of musical twangs as the piano's inner strings warped and snapped, succumbing to the face-melting heat.

Wiping a palmful of sweat from his forehead, Red shouted, "Thought you kids might be in trouble from the way you all ran by my trailer. But if I'd known it was *this* kinda trouble, I would've brought bigger fireworks!"

That makes two of us, I thought.

Just then, from the other side of the room, there came a deep rumbling sound: the cough and sputter of a huge combustion engine trying to turn over. No bueno.

"WHAT NOW?!" Ernie squealed.

"They're trying to get the piñata started!" shouted Liza.

Which meant that in less than thirty seconds, that gigantic, flame-spitting killer piñata bot was going to come lumbering on over to turn us into a platter of sangre-flavored chimichangas! I could practically see my tombstone now: JORGE LOPEZ, CAUSE OF DEATH—A FIRE-BREATHING CANDY DISPENSER. Talk about an embarrassing way to go!

Next thing I knew, Carter had leapt to his feet. "It's SupaCarter time!" he hissed, and before I could yell, "Carter, NO!" the fearless chupacabra was already running, already hopping over the piano, and already bounding straight for the mechanized piñata!

The bot's fiery eyes blazed as they locked on to the charging cryptid. Then its gigantic metal mouth screeched open, unleashing a blast of boiling blue-green flames that would've been pretty spectacular to behold if, of course, it hadn't been aimed *directly* at my best buddy!

Ernie and I let out bloodcurdling slasher movie shrieks. I mean, what did you expect us to do? It looked like Carter was about to become the world's hairiest french fry!

Fortunately, though, everyone's favorite bloodsucker was ready. With the kind of quicks that would've made a cheetah jealous, he ducked and dodged and suddenly leapt up, up, up—sailing through the air like a fur-covered hang glider!

His long, clawed fingers closed tightly around the

chain of a massive chandelier, and the chandelier swung out wide with his momentum, and then—

If you've ever busted open a piñata before, then you probably remember that exhilarating feeling when the papier-mâché finally splits open and the candy begins to drizzle down like sugary raindrops from heaven. Well, that's pretty much how I was feeling at the moment.

And honestly, I didn't even *care* that the piñata was raining nuts and bolts and shiny silver springs instead of Tootsie Rolls and lollipops!

We watched that overgrown candy dish stagger and stumble, teetering for a split second on its gigantic metal feet before finally crashing to the floor with the force of a collapsing building.

Leaping to my feet, I pumped my fist and shouted, "SHEEEOOOWWW!"

Chandelier drop for the win! And yeah, it was totally time for some good old-fashioned trash talk.

"Looks like we just sunk your battleship!" I shouted at Team Arsonist as Team Good Guys (that was us, by the way) laughed and cheered and exchanged high fives.

"That's a mighty fine animal you got there, son!" said Red, clapping me on the back. "A mighty fine animal!"

I grinned. "Thank you, sir! I really do love that

bloodsucker—er, I mean, pooch!"

No joke, it felt like we'd just won the FIFA World Cup! Actually, it felt even better, because instead of getting some silly golden trophy, we were getting to keep *our lives*!

Or so I'd thought . . .

Because just then, a familiar, slithery, villain-y voice spoke up behind us.

"You might have ended our piñata," it hissed. "But now I'm going to end all of *you*!"

CHAPTER 47

The four of us whirled around as a tall figure melted into view, its face half hidden in shadows. It was Kenneth—er, Elijah Blackbriar! His pale lips smirked cruelly at us, and the zzz-maker was steady as a rock in his hand.

I had about a split second to think, *¡Órale! Don't these zonzos ever quit?!* Then there came a high-pitched screech, followed by the crash of splintering wood—and the next thing I knew, the entire east wall of the ballroom exploded inward like somebody had set off a wagonful of dynamite on the other side!

Chunks of dusty plaster flew everywhere. The floorboards shuddered, and the whole rest of the wall came crashing down like an avalanche, burying the fire chief beneath a mountain of broken wood and stone.

For several seconds, nobody moved. Nobody even *breathed*. All I could figure was that some bad-tempered giant had decided to punch a hole in the side of the old Blackbriar mansion.

But as the dust slowly settled, and my shock slowly faded, I saw that it hadn't been a giant at all—

IT WAS A CHEVY LOWRIDER!!

Hey, hold up. I knew that Chevy . . .

And I knew its driver!

It was my abuela! My grandma had just plowed into Blackbriar Manor!

As I stood there, more stunned than a snowman in a bikini shop, the lowrider's doors flew open and out climbed my abuelos—my grandma clutching her trusty chancla as if it was the mighty Excalibur.

"GRANDMA? GRANDPA?" I burst out. "What are you doing here?!"

"Saving your butt!" she snapped. "What else?"

"Watch out!" Liza screamed, yanking us down as another volley of snooze darts came screaming this way.

I turned to Paz. "They're the ones behind the fires! Those are the arsonists! And over there's the piñata bot they've been using to scare the town!"

"I know that, dummy!" she said. "Red called us. Told us everything. ¡Y me los voy a comer vivos a todos!" And leaping to her feet she flung her chancla, Batarang-style, across the ballroom.

The deadly slipper whistled through the air like a perfectly thrown fastball and—

Man, now I know who I got my arm from! I thought, and I couldn't help but laugh.

"Hey, Mr. Wilson, I know Jorge's grandmother is super tough and all," Ernie shouted as another shower of darts whizzed by, "but please tell me you called the National Guard, too!"

Red shook his head. "Nah," he said, "but I called *them*."

As if on cue, there came the heavy clump of boots and I turned to see an army of police officers streaming into the war zone—er, *the ballroom*—through Paz's recently renovated entrance.

The officers had their batons and flashlights out and were shouting, "Everybody freeze!" and "Hands up!"

But apparently Team Arsonist wasn't planning on going down without a fight. They began slinging darts at the police, too, and even hit a couple!

Fortunately, not sixty seconds later, Boca's finest had them surrounded and had taken their dart slingers away. They slapped cuffs on good ole Benjamin Blackbriar even while he struggled and kicked and berated them with, "You can't do this to me! I'm the richest man in Boca! I own you! *I OWN THIS ENTIRE TOWN!*"

A few yards away, I found Paz standing grumpily over the dinged-up hood of her precious '64 Impala that she had just repaired. She frowned at a fist-size dent in the polished chrome fender and at the smoke rising from its shiny pink hood.

"That was some pretty nice driving there," I said, coming up beside her.

My abuela's frown deepened. "You better pray those golpes come out, or it's coming out of your allowance."

"But you don't even *give* me an allowance!" I pointed out.

"Then you better start looking for a job, 'cause somebody's paying for these repairs!"

That made me laugh. I was almost positive she was kidding. *Almost.* "Seriously, though. Can't believe you did that. You must really love me, huh?"

"*Love you?*" my abuela snapped. "Don't kid yourself, kid. I've just always wanted to drive my car through this place. Never liked it. Gives the whole town a creepy vibe."

Yep, that was Paz for ya.

Too bad for her, I could tell that she actually did love me.

CHAPTER 48

"Guess the fire chief was right!" Ernie grinned, hopping backward off a mossy old log. "You play with fire, you get burned."

The four of us (that's me, Liza, Ernie, and Carter) were sort of hanging out at the edge of the Blackbriar woods, waiting for my abuelos to finish giving their statements to the police so they could drive us home.

Farther away, by the grand east wing of the mansion, all the members of the Piñata Posse were being read their rights and shuffled into the back of squad cars even while the fire chief screamed, "You all are the true monsters! You'll pay for what you did to Miguel!" and Luna Thorne made a strong, final push for an insanity plea with, "But it's real! The piñata is *real*! The spirit of Miguel Valdez Blackbriar *lives*!"

Man, some people just don't know when to call it quits, do they?

"What a night, huh?" Liza said with an exhausted sigh.

"What a night? You mean, what a *week!*" cried Ernie with an even bigger sigh of exhaustion.

"You can say that again." I laughed. Honestly, it was kind of hard to wrap my brain around everything that had happened in the last few days. We'd done so much. Slipped out of some pretty tight spots. I mean, we'd found a way to keep the gang together. We'd befriended a misunderstood outcast, who, in the end, had turned out to be a literal lifesaver. We'd investigated an old local legend, saved the town from a fiery end, and somehow, someway, solved the decades-old case of the haunted piñata. It just goes to show that you should never—never *ever*—underestimate yourself. We're all way stronger and way smarter than we give ourselves credit for.

Sure, sometimes it might take a not-so-pleasant situation to bring out that strength and smartness. But it's in us all the same. You should also never underestimate what you and a few good friends can accomplish.

"Well, I don't know about everybody else," Ernie said, "but I'm kind of bummed."

"About what?" I asked.

"The whole piñata thing. The legend. Now that we know it was all a big crock of baloney, I kinda wish it was . . . true. Having a haunted piñata hanging around town would be sort of neat, I guess."

Liza glared at him. "*Neat?* Ernie, if there really was a haunted piñata hanging around Boca Falls, you'd never come out from under your bedcovers."

Ernie's shoulders went up and down like, *Eh, you're probably right,* and Liza said, "Anyway, so how are we going to celebrate our big win? Any ideas?"

"How 'bout slurpin' some fresh goat blood?" said Carter sincerely. "I know a nice little farm up the road. Some really friendly goats there."

Liza and Ernie exchanged total *Yikes!* looks, and I had a hard time wrestling down a laugh.

"Uh, how about we ask Paz if she can take us to grab some milkshakes on the way home instead?" I suggested. "We can go heavy on the cherry syrup."

At the mere mention of cherry syrup, Carter's stomach grumbled like a busted dishwasher and a big, fang-filled grin split his furry lips.

"I think that's a yes," Liza said with a smirk.

"A definite yes from me!" Ernie pitched in.

"Milkshakes it is!" I cheered.

Back by all the action, I saw Paz begin waving us impatiently over.

"Time to go," I said.

But no sooner had we all turned to start back toward the mansion than a strange sound drifted out of the dark woods. It was a low, hissing rattle— something like the world's creepiest maraca being shaken.

So, naturally, we all turned to look—

And I think it's pretty safe to say that none of us were prepared for what we *actually* saw . . .

The monster
does exist!

?!

Those monsters
do exist!

FIND OUT HOW IT ALL BEGAN!

Read Jorge and Carter's first adventure:

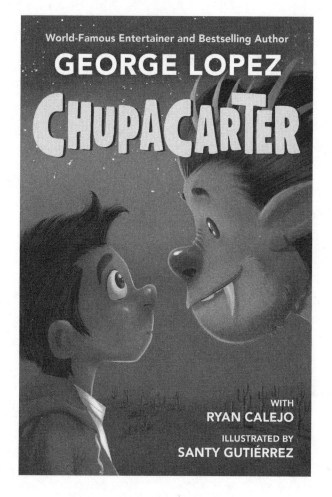